She knew what his *next* step would be

Cal stumbled as he jumped across the water to the next boulder. Automatically Juniper's hand shot out to steady him.

"Thanks," he murmured.

Somehow her hand refused to leave his arm. "Wouldn't want to have to scrape you off the rocks."

"Why, Juniper, what a romantic thought."

Romance, of course, was exactly what she needed to avoid. But anything Cal said in that low, sandpapery voice was bound to make her pulse race.

"Juniper, why are you trying to destroy the mood?"

"Because otherwise—" she was breathless despite herself "—we might kiss or something. And neither of us wants that."

Cal laughed softly, his gaze going to her fingers, and she realized they were caressing him. "Let's say we start with a kiss, then see what we both want after that...."

Carla Neggers is one of seven children, so she knows all about the ties that bind. Which could be why she handles the family shenanigans in *Trade Secrets* with such aplomb. Carla's gift for writing clever dialogue, as well as her delightful sense of fun, are also major strengths; well established in the romance genre, she has eighteen novels to her credit. Carla lives with her husband and family in Massachusetts, but she has a soft spot for northern Maine. Every year she vacations there, in a cottage similar to the one in which her characters find romance.

Books by Carla Neggers

CLAIM THE CROWN

HARLEQUIN TEMPTATION
108–CAPTIVATED

Don't miss any of our special offers. Write to us at the following address for information on our newest releases.

Harlequin Reader Service
901 Fuhrmann Blvd., P.O. Box 1397, Buffalo, NY 14240
Canadian address: P.O. Box 603,
Fort Erie, Ont. L2A 5X3

Published July 1987

ISBN 0-373-25262-5

Trade Secrets

CARLA NEGGERS

Harlequin Books

TORONTO • NEW YORK • LONDON
AMSTERDAM • PARIS • SYDNEY • HAMBURG
STOCKHOLM • ATHENS • TOKYO • MILAN

1

HE DIDN'T BELONG. Even from across the lawn, from among the red tulips, Juniper Killibrew could see that. For one thing, if he'd belonged she would have known who he was. After all, she knew everyone else who'd been invited to the annual tulip festival on the sprawling grounds of Killibrew Traders, Inc. For another, if he'd belonged he'd have been wearing at least one article of clothing from a Killibrew Traders catalog. Everyone else was. *He* wore faded, close-fitting jeans— not a Killibrew item—and a simple, loosely cut cotton shirt, wine-colored, definitely not a Killibrew item.

No, he didn't belong.

Unexpectedly he caught her eye and, just as unexpectedly, grinned. Juniper glanced down at a cluster of tulips and pretended not to notice either the flash of his eyes in her direction or, particularly, the grin. She would be cool, she decided, if still outrageously curious.

As she sipped her tart, fresh-squeezed lemonade, she considered who the stranger might be. A new model for the men's catalog, perhaps? Extremely unlikely. No. Impossible. Absolutely not. There were streaks of gray in his dark hair and too many odd angles to his face— she could see that even from her position. His shoulders were too broad, his chest too deep and his legs too long. He was striking, although not handsome, maybe not even good looking, but certainly *not* model material. Potential customers would look at him and not give a damn about the clothes he wore.

As it was, Juniper had only noticed his clothes because she was paid to notice such details, *bred* to. Like it or not, she was a Killibrew.

Stealing a glance back at the outsider, she saw him moving in her direction. He might detour at any moment, of course, but she had a feeling he wouldn't. And it wouldn't matter, in any case. She would just wander on over to him. She wanted to know who he was.

A gate-crasher? Now that was entirely more likely than a male model, although he didn't look the least bit concerned about being discovered, and he hadn't loaded up his plate with food. In fact, she hadn't seen him eat or drink anything, and she'd been observing him, quietly and inconspicuously, of course, for the past fifteen minutes. She'd begun to refer to him as her Man in Jeans.

Just as he was about to round a bed of multicolored tulips, another man approached him. Juniper gulped her lemonade. Damn! But there he was: Summerfield Killibrew. They chatted a minute or two, and her Man in Jeans threw back his head and laughed. Echoes of his amusement reached her ears. It was a rich, full-bodied laugh but, then, she'd expected nothing less.

And he was a friend of Summerfield's. A pity.

Juniper turned away in annoyance and, she had to admit, disappointment. Well, what else could she expect to feel but disappointment? Summerfield was her uncle, her senior by only nine years—and nothing if not conceited, lazy, irresponsible and utterly feckless. In short, he had the makings of what Auntie Killibrew would call a rogue. "All Killibrew men are rogues," she had told her grandniece countless times.

At least, Juniper thought, Uncle Summerfield was wearing Killibrew Traders clothes, albeit that the bright green poplins and madras shirt were not her favorites. She preferred his friend's worn jeans.

"Horrors," she muttered to herself, and laughed.

She herself was dressed in Traders linen separates—white pleated skirt, fuchsia jacket, pale pink camp shirt. They were on page forty of the women's catalog and a fringe benefit of being vice president of marketing and sales. Her hair was ash blond, short and carefully highlighted, and her coloring was cool, her eyes a clear gray, "saucer eyes," Auntie used to call them. She was of medium height but appeared taller because of her long legs, although she refused to wear heels more than an inch and a half high.

"Enjoying yourself?"

She jumped, slightly startled by the voice close behind her. It was deep and liquid, and as she turned, she saw her Man in Jeans. Naturally he would be the silent-approach type. She smiled, retaining her composure despite the man's assault on her senses. Up close, he was everything she'd anticipated—and perhaps more. "Yes," she said calmly, "I always enjoy the festival."

He smiled back, a rakish smile that prompted her gaze to travel quickly over him and soak up additional details now that he was standing so close. She took in the tiny scar at the corner of his mouth and the slightly crooked nose, telling her he'd been in a brawl at some point in his no doubt checkered past. And the eyes. They were surprisingly light under such thick dark eyebrows, and a clear cornflower blue. Probably they could twinkle if he wanted them to—and look sensual at the same time, as they did now. But those eyes wouldn't twinkle at her. No, she thought, never. She hadn't had a man's eyes twinkle at her in—oh, she couldn't remember. Maybe never. She'd never gone in for the silly, manipulative antics that seemed to amuse so many men, at least the kind she generally met on a casual basis. The kind, she added silently, feeling slightly rebellious, who wore Killibrew Traders clothes.

"Then this isn't your first time here," he said.

If he was putting the moves on her, she thought, he was being deliciously subtle. She wasn't one for the caveman approach. Probably, though, he was just making conversation. Being polite. Summerfield had asked him to, no doubt. She frowned. If that was the case, her Man in Jeans certainly knew she was a Killibrew.

"Oh, no," she said.

Although she couldn't pinpoint why, Juniper was grateful that her uncle hadn't identified her as his sourpuss niece, the brains of the family. Her Man in Jeans still gave no indication of knowing who she was. For the past six years she had had the unenviable responsibility not only of performing her expected duties as vice president, but also of filling in for Summerfield. Trying, without success, to get him to pay attention to his company. He was president and chief executive officer of Killibrew Traders, by virtue of owning a majority of its stock, and she had to put up with him, since she owned no stock in the company. Her father, Summerfield's much older brother, had seen to that. Feckless, lovable rogue like the rest of them, he'd put all his

profits into a hospital boat so that he and his doctor-
wife could sail the South Seas and bring medicine to the
impoverished. He'd always maintained that Juniper had
enough guts and intelligence to get along without some
ridiculous inheritance. Since Summerfield clearly
couldn't get along without her, she'd never worried. Job
security was at rock bottom of her worry list.

"Do you work at Killibrew?" her Man in Jeans asked.

She sat down on a stone bench in front of a bed of
tulips and set her lemonade glass on the arm. There was
room for him to sit beside her, but he didn't. Instead he
propped his foot on the bench and leaned forward over
his knee, looking out at the tulips. It was a perfect May
afternoon in New Hampshire, and Juniper wondered if
she just might have a touch of spring fever—highly unlike her.

"Yes, I work there," she said vaguely. "Are you a
friend of Summerfield's? I saw you speaking with him."

"I didn't think anyone called him Summerfield," her
Man in Jeans said with a grin. There was a deep, hor-
izontal line in his forehead, and his teeth were even and
well spaced. He had all the makings of one of Auntie's
rogues, Juniper realized, amused. He went on. "Yes,
we're friends. Sum's quite a character."

Delicately put. But Juniper didn't want to get into a
discussion of her uncle's numerous faults. She looked
up at her stranger and sighed at the way the sunlight
sparkled in his eyes, and she wondered if he was noticing anything about *her* eyes. He didn't seem to be. What
were they talking about? Oh, Summerfield, of course.
"He has his moments," she said judiciously. "Are you
staying for the jazz band?"

Every year the tulip festival promised two things: plenty of food and jazz. Everything else—the weather, the number of attendees, even the presence of tulips—couldn't be counted on. One year the tulips had all gone by in an unusually warm spring. The next year they hadn't yet opened in an unusually cool one. But this year everything was turning out as it was meant to, and by five o'clock the jazz band would begin to perform.

But her Man in Jeans shook his head. "No, I can't stay. I'm afraid I have to be back in New York tonight."

She was surprised by her disappointment. "Will Summerfield be going with you?"

"No, he said it's his duty to stay here."

She almost laughed: what did Summerfield Killibrew know of duty?

"He's coming down to Newport next weekend. He's going to crew for me. Why don't you come, too?"

The man didn't even know her name, but he was already inviting her places. Well, she could see why he and her uncle got along! Such spontaneity had never been her long suit. But she wished she didn't feel such a rush of warmth—of outrageous temptation. *Don't take him seriously,* she warned herself. *You're the sensible Killibrew, remember?* "Then you're on vacation?"

He laughed. "Some people would say I'm always on vacation."

Yes, definitely a Summerfield ally. Best to make an exit now before her touch of spring fever turned into an uncontrollable seizure. Sighing with regret, she excused herself and, not waiting for his response, went off for more lemonade. Fresh-squeezed lemonade, very lightly sweetened, was another tradition of the festival, one Juniper insisted upon maintaining, not because she didn't trust her guests with anything stronger, but because she didn't trust her family.

Auntie Killibrew joined her at the cooler. Somewhere in her seventies—her age and her real first name being her two most closely guarded secrets—Auntie had shrunk somewhat from her original five foot eleven inches, but she was still an imposing figure. Juniper couldn't see much of her strong, lined face under the ancient, wide-brimmed straw hat. She was wearing a Traders navy-blue linen dress from a catalog of some forty years ago.

"He's a rogue," Auntie said.

Juniper didn't bother to look around. "Who?"

"The man over there. Look at those eyes, that smile. The devil himself would tiptoe around such a man."

"Oh, Auntie." Juniper laughed. Her elderly aunt was an avid observer of people, and she liked to sum up their character in two sentences or less. She was often deadly accurate.

Then Juniper's Man in Jeans strolled past them with a single red tulip in his hand—picking the tulips was absolutely forbidden—and gave Juniper a disarming grin. She found herself grinning back and started to wave, but caught Auntie's knowing look. So *he* was Auntie's rogue! Juniper stopped short and turned back to the lemonade, chuckling to herself. She couldn't very well have Auntie finding out that her grandniece had been chatting with a bona fide rogue.

But Auntie was pursing her lips, her look one of uneasy resignation. Of all the eccentric Killibrews, Auntie was Juniper's favorite. "It's the fate of Killibrew women to fall for rogues, Juniper," the elderly woman pronounced. "But you mustn't blame yourself. It's in your genes. There's simply nothing to be done about it."

Juniper pulled her gaze from the retreating jean-clad figure and straightened. "We'll see about that."

Perhaps it was just as well he was departing for New York. The spring New England air was getting to her, or was *he* to blame? Perhaps he'd really been serious about having her slip off to Newport next weekend.

"Good heavens," she mumbled to herself, "don't be absurd!"

Without a doubt he'd issued the very same invitation to half the women at the festival. Juniper poured herself another glass of lemonade and got away quickly from Auntie Killibrew's persistent, knowing look.

But Auntie needn't worry. Whatever else her Man in Jeans might be, he was clearly a friend of Summerfield's. And that was enough to make Juniper keep her distance.

IN THE OFFICE of the president and chief executive officer of Killibrew Traders, which overlooked the dwindling crowd at the tulip festival, Summerfield Killibrew offered his friend, Calvin Gilliam, a drink. "You're sure no one knows you haven't left?" Sum asked.

Cal took the offered Scotch and seated himself in front of Sum's immaculate desk. The office was done in muted grays, more subdued, Cal thought, than Sum himself. But despite his eccentricities, Sum was a complex individual, not easily pegged. Although they'd known each other a relatively short time, perhaps eighteen months, Cal considered him one of his most trusted friends, which was why he was willing to go along with him now.

"Don't worry," Cal said. "I've let it be known among the guests that I have to be back in New York tonight."

Sum nodded, but he was still visibly nervous, and understandably so, in Cal's opinion. Cal had tried to talk him into considering other means to the same intended end, but Sum was convinced that his was the only way. He was a tawny-haired man of medium build with a square jaw, pale eyes and a straight nose. There was something about him that reminded Cal of the cool and lovely woman he'd visited with among the red tulips, but given Sum's peculiarities and the blonde's straitlaced manner, Cal couldn't imagine that they were related. In fact, he wasn't sure why he'd gone over to her in the first place. He'd told himself he had just wanted to pass the word about his leaving the festival early, but he could have accomplished that in any of a dozen different ways. There must have been something about her that had drawn him across the lawn. Her laughing gray eyes? Or just that he'd caught her staring at him and couldn't resist?

"What about your car?" Sum inquired, still worried.

"It's parked down the road. I don't think anyone will notice it—or saw me in it." Cal smiled reassuringly. "It doesn't have my name on it, you know."

Sum ran a hand through his hair and sighed heavily. "Sorry to seem so paranoid, but if the wrong people get wind of our meeting . . ."

Cal shrugged. "It's your company, Sum. You can do as you please."

"I know, but—*damn*." He plopped down in the leather chair behind his desk and sat there stiffly, as if he didn't belong—which, in a way, he didn't. He'd told

Cal that from the beginning. "Well, you've had your look around. What do you think?"

"My opinion hasn't changed," Cal said, businesslike once more. "Killibrew Traders is a well-run, profitable company, and my offer stands firm."

Sum didn't look as relieved as he might have, rather more guilty than anything. Again Cal could hardly blame him. What Summerfield Killibrew was taking was a tremendous risk, both personally and financially, but it seemed to Cal that his friend had been looking for exactly this opportunity all his life. "Then we can begin drawing up the papers?" Sum asked.

Cal Gilliam smiled. "I already have."

"There's . . ." Sum glanced sideways, out the window, where the sun was setting on the lush Killibrew lawns and the thousands of tulips that had opened up under the warm spring sun. "Cal, there's only one thing I feel I should warn you about."

"Yes?"

Sum licked his lips. "My niece."

Cal laughed. "Your niece? What, does she toddle up to her uncle's office every day looking for a lollipop?"

"Hardly. She's only nine years younger than I am and happens to be vice president of marketing and sales. Cal, she's been running the place."

This piqued Cal's interest, and he leaned forward, elbows resting on his thighs. "Juniper Killibrew. I saw her name and guessed she might be a relative. Why haven't you mentioned her before?"

"Repression."

"She doesn't own any stock. Why worry about her?"

Sum breathed heavily, guiltily, and hunched his shoulders as if warding off something very unpleasant. "I haven't done right by her, Cal, especially lately. Juniper's worked her butt off . . . and for damned little gratitude from me."

"So I'll treat her well," Cal said, unworried. "Sum, she must have reconciled herself by now to not being a stockholder. If she's as savvy as you say, she'll realize she has no voice in what you do with your own company. I have no intention of interfering with her. So I repeat: why should I worry about her?"

Summerfield Killibrew ran one finger along the edge of a virtually unused blotter. "She might get a bit irritated about my selling the family company."

"It's not the family company—hasn't been for years. It's your company. She'll get over it."

"Maybe. She could also quit."

"So? I'll hire someone else. Sum, one person isn't going to make or break Killibrew Traders. If she's unhappy, she can leave."

Sum looked doubtful. "The company's growth during the past three years has been her doing, Cal. I can't pretend otherwise. She's a damned good executive, and she *cares* about Killibrew Traders—a hell of a lot more than I ever have."

"So I'll persuade her to stay." Cal leaned back in the cozy chair, drumming up concern only for Sum's sake. He'd dealt with hostile vice presidents before. And he always prevailed in the end. "What's our Juniper Killibrew like?"

Her uncle could only inhale deeply and grimly shake his head. "I don't know, Cal. I guess she's like her namesake plant—prickly and poisonous."

2

IT WAS DUSK when Juniper finally made her way through the woods, following the grassy path she had trotted along since childhood. Wide, picturesque and flanked by two-hundred-year-old stone walls, it led from the back lawns of Killibrew Traders through a five-acre patch of woods to what was left of Summerfield House, where Juniper lived. It was a rambling, drafty Victorian, built by Great-Grandfather Summerfield back when the Summerfields had been among the shoe kings of the Northeast. *That* had changed, of course. Grandpa Killibrew, Great-Grandfather Summerfield's grandson, had bailed out of Summerfield Shoe in the nineteen-thirties and had used the profits to launch Killibrew Traders.

Juniper breathed deeply of the cool evening air, soaking in the freshness of the woods. She would never understand her family, she supposed. After the death of his wife in the mid-sixties, Grandpa Killibrew had turned over his interest in Killibrew Traders to his two sons and left for parts unknown. He hadn't been heard from since. Popular myth had him eaten by crocodiles in the Amazon while rescuing some beautiful damsel.

More likely, Juniper thought, he'd gotten himself lost and ended up in the stew pot of some unfriendly natives. Rogues didn't come to heroic ends—not in her scheme of things.

If Summerfield Shoe, long owned by outsiders, was now nearly bankrupt, Killibrew Traders was thriving. And Summerfield House was on the mend. Juniper had bought the wreck of a place and was slowly renovating it.

Feeling it her duty, she had stayed at the festival until the last of the guests had left, the band had packed up and the cleaning crew had arrived. Now she appreciated the solitude and quiet of the woods and the light smells of spring. She was looking forward to getting back to her impossible house, where she had lived, alone but for two cats and a dog, for the past eighteen months. Thus far her renovations had amounted to discovering there were nine layers of wallpaper in the living room. She'd also bought a new refrigerator.

All at once her pace slackened. Smack in the middle of the path, where it dipped close to the main road and joined another track, there was a pearl-gray Mercedes 450SL. A bird had left a white splotch on the sparkling windshield. As she circled to the rear of the car, Juniper noted the Virginia license plate.

Virginia. How unexpected.

The tires of the driver's side were parked on Killibrew Traders property; those on the passenger side were parked on Juniper Killibrew's property. She peered through the windows. There was a black leather jacket tossed carelessly on the passenger seat that gave her a strange feeling, almost a quiver, in the small of her back. But there was nothing suspicious. No dead bodies, no illicit drugs, no smooching teenagers. Not that many teenagers would be driving such an expensive sports car, but one never knew.

An organized person, Juniper whisked out her leather-covered date book and jotted down the license number and make of the car.

"You look like a meter maid," the voice of the Man in Jeans drawled behind her.

She flipped her date book shut. "I believe they're called parking violation officers now."

He smiled without showing any teeth. "I'll have to remember that."

"Aren't you supposed to be in New York?"

"I was delayed."

She tucked her date book back in her handbag. "I didn't notice you lingering at the festival. Where did you go?"

He hesitated, just for a second, but that was long enough for Juniper to become suspicious. "I went for a walk," he said.

Liar, she thought—not that he owed her the truth, she reminded herself. This would be the last item Auntie Killibrew would need to confirm that the man was a rogue. In Auntie's book, all rogues were liars. Recalling that Summerfield, too, had disappeared early, Juniper, always alert to negative undercurrents, felt her interest perk up even more. Unfortunately, her skepticism didn't have a corresponding dampening effect on her spring fever: her Man in Jeans still seemed pretty sexy to her. She attempted to look uninterested. "Why did you park all the way out here?" she asked.

He leaned against the side of the car and folded his arms across his chest, almost as if he himself had decided to look the part of the rogue. Neither her questions nor his lies seemed to perturb him. "It's a romantic spot."

"What bilge," Juniper nearly scoffed. She didn't bother to look to see if his eyes were twinkling. "You're trespassing," she said tartly.

"Oh?"

"Not that I mind, but at this very moment half your car and all of you are on Killibrew property."

"Killibrew Traders—"

She straightened up and adopted her haughtiest look. "*Juniper* Killibrew's property. Mine."

Something strangely like panic flickered across his angular face, but she knew that couldn't be the case. Rogues never panicked. Whatever it was, it only lasted an instant before he swore to himself. "Hell." He walked around to the other side of the car. Safely on Killibrew Traders property, he opened the driver's door. "A pleasure meeting you, Ms Killibrew."

His sudden formality didn't work. Considering the faded jeans, the elegant car, the liquid drawl and the surrounding woods, the attempt to distance himself, to be formal and polite, seemed at best out of place. In a way, another lie. She wondered if discovering she was a Killibrew had brought on the manners. Did he know she was vice president? Perhaps he was only out scouting for a job.

Her gaze fell to the expensive car. No, she thought, that wasn't at all likely.

He was climbing into the driver's seat. "By the way," she called quickly, "what's your name?"

Pretending not to hear her, he shut the door. He didn't look at her, but she stood watching as he started the car and backed it quickly and skillfully down toward the main road.

"Hmm," she muttered to herself, imitating Auntie. Obviously the Man in Jeans didn't want her to be Juniper Killibrew.

What had Summerfield told him?

The moment she reached her kitchen, drenched in the fiery light of sunset, Juniper called her dear, sweet, conniving Uncle Summerfield.

"I want to know who he is," she said.

"Who who is?"

He already sounded guilty. With her extra-long telephone cord, Juniper paced. "Dark hair, jeans, wine-colored shirt, gray Mercedes 450SL, Virginia license plate, seen with you at the festival. Said he had to be in New York this evening and isn't. Sneaky. Now. His name, Uncle."

"Juniper, Juniper—"

"His name."

Summerfield sighed. "Calvin Gilliam."

Juniper sank momentarily against her refrigerator at this worst-possible news, but then rallied and kicked a tacky metal cabinet. "The raider?"

"So—" she could sense her uncle's discomfort "—so you've heard of him, huh, June?"

"Of course. What kind of idiot do you take me for? I read the *Wall Street Journal*, Summerfield. Calvin Gilliam buys and sells whatever he can—including people, if they'll let him."

"That's an exaggeration."

"And he's your friend, isn't he?"

"Well . . ."

She groaned. "Oh, Summerfield. When will you learn?"

"He's a good guy, Juniper."

She snorted. "He's an unscrupulous rogue!"

"Did he . . . you and he . . . What did you two do?"

"Summerfield!"

"Sorry. I should have known. You're not Cal's type, anyway."

"What's that supposed to mean?"

"You know."

She supposed, at age thirty-one, she ought to. Although her eccentric great-aunt might think her niece was fated to be attracted to the roguish type, it didn't necessarily follow that the roguish type would be attracted to her. Not that she *was* attracted to rogues, she reminded herself. Certainly not to Calvin Gilliam.

But who was she kidding? She thought of his light cornflower eyes and his rakish grin, and she had to admit there were certain undeniable physical attractions to the man. But anger had cleared her head: she'd never been interested in the merely physical. Much to her occasional distress, that was something she had always known.

"Summerfield," she said briskly, "please be careful. You're a nice person, and Calvin Gilliam isn't. I wouldn't want him to take advantage of you."

Her uncle quietly told her he had to go, wished her a good-night and hung up.

And left his niece and vice president in her kitchen, standing and thinking he hadn't begun to tell her the truth.

Something was wrong. Desperately wrong.

CAL GILLIAM TOOK a long shower the minute he arrived at the elegant Portsmouth inn where he was spending the night. It had been a close call with Juniper Killibrew—too close. He had been drawn to her wide, round gray eyes and cool ash-blond hair and to her obvious wit and intelligence. But he hadn't guessed, there among the tulips, that she was *the* Juniper Killibrew. The bottom-line, brass-tacks brilliant vice president of Killibrew Traders. The prickly and poisonous niece.

He should have guessed. There was that strong family resemblance between her and her uncle, and who the devil else could she have been, given his present luck, but vice president of the company he was about to buy? It had been that way with Sum's scheme from the beginning. Lots of trouble and too damned much sneaking around.

Well, at least he'd made his escape before he'd done any more damage. But sooner or later he was going to have to deal with Ms Juniper Killibrew—and he didn't think either of them was going to like it.

When the telephone rang, he snatched it up on the first ring.

"She knows who you are," Sum said without preliminary.

Cal sighed irritably. "That didn't take long."

"I think she's suspicious."

"A state of mind for her since birth, I should imagine."

"Cal, this isn't a joke. I *can't* have her finding out about the sale at this stage. God knows what she'd do to stop me. Look—are you registered under an assumed name?"

"Of course not. Sum, don't you think you're overreacting?"

"No."

"Why not just sit the woman down and explain to her what's happening and why?"

"I can't. She'd talk me out of it."

That was an understatement, Cal had to admit. More likely she'd tie Sum up in a closet and tell the world he'd gone mad—or disappeared—like his legendary father. Cal asked dryly, "She's not your heir, is she?"

"Lord, I'm not *that* stupid."

"Well, I'll do what I can to keep this quiet. I'm sorry your niece and I had a run-in, but she's just that sort of woman. But I agreed to present your staff with a fait accompli of the sale of the company, and I'll stick by that."

"Thanks, Cal."

"And I'll get out of town at first light."

THE INN WHERE CALVIN GILLIAM was staying topped the list Juniper had made up, because it was the best one in town. She also knew the innkeeper, who told her the notorious individual had reserved his room more than a week before. And that meant someone was keeping something from her.

Calvin Gilliam had never intended to leave the festival early, and he had parked his car in an out-of-the-way place for a reason.

Had he and Summerfield cooked up some kind of scheme?

Don't be naive, Juniper. Of course they have!

But who, she thought, was using whom?

She sat down to a glass of milk and a stack of graham crackers, which, she hoped, would calm her stomach. As usual, there was no one she could call. Summerfield had already lied, and she could only anticipate more of the same. Her parents were somewhere in the South Pacific. Her sister, Sage, was off in the Rockies teaching troubled teenagers how to rely on their inner resources. Auntie would be no help whatsoever. "Fall in love with the man," she'd say. "It's your fate." And Grandpa Killibrew was God only knew where.

She called in Bo, her unintelligent, mostly golden retriever mutt, gathered her cats on her lap and told them all that she was afraid her trusting Uncle Summerfield had gotten himself involved with the wrong kind of person. And this time she didn't know if she could bail him out in time.

They all responded by rolling over on their backs so she could scratch their stomachs. Could she possibly be seeing a conspiracy where none existed? Impossible. She had a nose for such things.

She thought of her Man in Jeans. Calvin Gilliam, the notorious corporate raider. And if nothing else, she supposed she should have known. Auntie was right: the devil himself would tiptoe around such a man.

"But not me," Juniper said aloud. "Juniper Killibrew doesn't tiptoe around anyone."

3

DURING THE NEXT TWO WEEKS the tulips went by, and the leaves budded, and Juniper slowly, warily permitted her state of alert to ease. Summerfield had left Portsmouth the Monday after the festival and hadn't been heard from since, which was par for the course. Juniper could run Killibrew Traders as she pleased without having to worry about trying to get her uncle to act more like an executive and less like a Killibrew.

But, more important, Calvin Gilliam had checked out of the elegant New England inn the Sunday after the festival, and *he* hadn't been heard from since. Juniper had tried without success to find out if he and Summerfield had gone sailing in Newport the following weekend, but her Newport and sailing contacts were abysmally inadequate. In her present state of optimism, she decided that clue had been another of Calvin Gilliam's lies. Could it be, she thought, that this one time Summerfield had actually heeded her advice? Or perhaps she'd been too suspicious this once.

Having stopped to buy putty knives and sponges to inspire her to begin removing the layers of old wallpaper in the living room, Juniper arrived at her office late Monday morning. Yet she felt energetic and in control of her own destiny. She was wearing her classic blue seersucker suit from page sixty-five of the women's catalog.

Her secretary, Beth, an efficient woman of thirty who was five months pregnant with her second child, met Juniper anxiously as she breezed into the office. "You'd better hurry," Beth said. "The meeting's already started."

Juniper frowned. She prided herself on never forgetting a meeting. "It's not on my schedule."

"Er—no. It's an emergency meeting of all management personnel."

"What!"

There was only one person who could have called such a meeting without her knowledge: the president and chief executive officer of Killibrew Traders.

Dear, sweet conniving Summerfield. Her uncle.

In Juniper's six years with the company, Summerfield Killibrew had never been known to call *any* meeting.

With great forboding, Juniper rushed down to the conference room and burst through the double doors.

Calvin Gilliam was standing at the head of the conference table with her uncle. Her Man in Jeans. Only today Gilliam was in a crisp, tailored khaki suit, looking every bit the part of the corporate raider. Juniper stood motionless, suspended. She didn't think she was breathing. And at first she heard nothing. She only saw the tall man with the clear blue eyes and the striking, sexy looks. She might have seen him only moments before, not two weeks, so vivid was her recollection of every detail of his face, his body, the sound of his voice. There was no roguish grin today. He was all business. And yet he somehow still looked so casually in control, irreverent, unconcerned about the opinions of the people around him.

Their eyes met briefly, his cool, hers blazing, and he inclined his head ever so slightly, acknowledging her presence, possibly even reading her mind.

Summerfield was at his side, in full Killibrew Traders regalia of gray gabardine. At last Juniper became aware of what her uncle was saying. "As new owner, Calvin Gilliam will be committed to the same standards of excellence—"

"*No!*" she yelled.

"As has been the tradition of Killibrew Traders for the past half century." Summerfield refused to look at his niece.

Juniper swallowed a curse as she fought to retain her composure. She went rigid and balled her hands into fists at her sides, willing herself to respond to this piracy as a professional. The news was worse than even she had imagined possible. As new owner... Oh, Lord! But knowing Summerfield as she unfortunately did and aware of Calvin Gilliam's reputation as she undoubtedly was, Juniper suspected they were presenting the staff with a fait accompli.

Killibrew Traders had already been sold to the Raider Gilliam, and there wasn't anything she could do about it. They would have already seen to that.

"You sneaky bastards." She almost choked on the words then about-faced and stormed from the conference room.

In her white-and-mauve office, she stood at her window but didn't see the bright spring sunshine dancing on the lush lawns. She didn't feel betrayed. Summerfield wasn't devious enough to betray anyone, let alone his own niece, and Calvin Gilliam owed her nothing whatsoever and therefore couldn't betray her. No,

Summerfield simply hadn't told her his plans because he knew she'd object—because he'd been afraid she'd talk some sense into him, or at least appeal to his sense of duty and honor. He had precious little of either, but she might have been able to do *something* had she known what was about to unfold.

She wanted to slam her fist into the window but held back. Damn them both. How much had Gilliam paid for the company? It had to have been in the millions.

"Oh, Summerfield," she moaned.

Juniper felt that she herself had failed, and failed profoundly. She had known for years that Summerfield, like his brother and father and various ancestors before him, had a yearning to do something out of the ordinary. It was in his blood, a genetic quirk. She'd known he wanted to bail out of Killibrew Traders—like his father, like his brother. She had worked tirelessly to keep the company profitable and well respected. She had tried so hard to interest him in the catalog clothing business, in family honor, if nothing else. Instead he was following family tradition: selling out and damn whom it hurt.

When he had decided he'd had enough—she had known the day would come—Juniper had hoped at least to be in a position to buy a controlling interest and keep Killibrew Traders in the family.

But obviously, such was not to be the case.

She shut her eyes, angry and miserable. She was the last of the Killibrews of Killibrew Traders, and she owned no stock, had no stake in the company, would from here on out be at the beck and call of a non-Killibrew, a man who had no interest in the company beyond the profits it would net him—a bona fide rogue, as Auntie had warned. She was a salaried employee. What was the point?

She buzzed Beth, who had just returned from her coffee break with her daughter, a four-year-old rapscallion who stayed in the company's day-care facility while her mother and father, who was in quality control, worked. The family had lunch together, and during her afternoon break Beth liked to go down and push her daughter on the swings. It was a nice arrangement for both parents, and since instituting on-site quality day care and liberal parental leaves, Juniper had noticed a marked decrease in employee absenteeism. Strictly speaking, such policies weren't her province, but who was there to stop her? Certainly not Summerfield, who was gone so much....

Calvin Gilliam. What all would he demand be dismantled?

"What can I do for you, Juniper?" Beth asked.

"I need you to take a letter. To my parents. I think they're somewhere in the Philippines; I'll get you the address. Actually, make it a telegram. Word it yourself. Tell them Summerfield's off his rocker and I need all the support I can get to block the sale of Killibrew Traders to a pirate." She threw up her hands in frustration. "I have to at least *try* to do something!"

But as Beth noted her instructions, Calvin Gilliam darkened her doorway, literally. He blocked out the morning sun that was streaming in from the outer office. In spite of everything, Juniper took a sharp breath of awareness. He was one very noticeable man. He placed a hand high up on the doorframe. "It won't work," he said.

Stiffening at his casual tone, Juniper nodded to Beth. "Go ahead and send the cable."

Beth retreated with a nervous smile at Gilliam, whose gaze remained on Juniper. He wasn't smiling, but still looked maddeningly calm, and therefore all the more insensitive. He had no idea, or simply didn't care, what he and Summerfield had just done to the life of Juniper Killibrew. She could have thrown something at him but instead stayed rigidly at her desk.

Gilliam took a couple of steps into the office, then leaned back against the wall near the door and put one foot out in front of him, a stance that was at once lazy and arrogant. He was studying her without any apparent effort to disguise that he was doing so, which annoyed her more than anything else. She was too shocked and angry to feel self-conscious.

"If you'll excuse me," she said sharply, "I have business to tend to."

"The sale's final, Juniper."

Juniper. Her name just rolled off his tongue.

"There's not a thing you can do to stop it. Sum's seen to that."

"And I suppose you haven't done a thing."

He gave just the barest hint of a smile, which had the effect of rubbing salt in her wounds. "I've tried to stay in the background and let him handle this as he has felt necessary."

"Ha." Juniper leaned back in her chair. Hard. "A reputation for truthfulness and integrity does *not* precede you, Mr. Gilliam."

He ignored her jibe and drew away from the wall, moving toward her. "Obviously, since the sale has gone through, it won't be necessary for me to remain in the background any longer." The smile vanished, replaced by an intensity that most people, Juniper thought, would find difficult to meet head-on. She merely rested back in her chair, unimpressed. "Juniper," he continued, "I want you to know that I have no intention of interfering with the running of Killibrew Traders. I'm well aware of your talents. You've been in charge here for some time, and you've done an incredible job. I don't want that to change."

She snorted. "I'll bet you don't!"

He stopped abruptly and stared at her in surprise. "I beg your pardon?"

"Considering the growth of Killibrew Traders in recent years, you'd be a fool if you wanted to change a thing." She looked at him levelly. "And whatever else you are, Calvin Gilliam, you're certainly no fool."

He stood in front of her desk and placed his hands on the outer edge, leaning toward her. In spite of herself she was aware of every muscle, every hard line in his extraordinary face. "Then you'll stay?"

"If I were you, Mr. Gilliam," she said, her tone cool as she met his eyes, "I wouldn't ask me that right now. I'd wait until some of the shock and anger had worn off. Right now I'm extremely annoyed and likely to strike out in any way I can."

The corners of his mouth twitched. "I see."

"I suggest you leave."

"Back off, you mean?"

"The sooner the better."

"Good advice."

"Ask my uncle—I'm known for it."

He tapped her blotter with one finger. "So he warned me. I'll be in touch, Juniper Killibrew."

She watched him leave. If a stride could show concern, then Calvin Gilliam wasn't the least bit concerned. He walked with the same air of calm with which he had strolled about the tulip festival in his jeans two weeks before. Nothing bothered him.

Pushing her chair back from her desk, Juniper exhaled loudly. So the new owner of Killibrew Traders appreciated her talents, wanted her to stay, was even willing to walk on eggshells around her—at least for now. Was he afraid of her? That amused her, but only because he was Calvin Gilliam. Ordinarily she preferred to inspire respect, not fear.

Oh, but that was ridiculous, Calvin Gilliam was anything but afraid. What a clever man he was. Coming on—or trying to—as the desperate and kindhearted new owner, a man who needed her executive talents. Demanding from her a measured, professional response, when he undoubtedly knew full well that what she wanted to do was break a chair over his head. She had seen through his tactics, of course. "Rogues are eminently transparent," Auntie had always maintained.

Well, Juniper thought, she'd give Cal Gilliam his measured, professional response—but not because he or Summerfield deserved it. She was thinking of the employees of Killibrew Traders. For their sake, she wouldn't act on impulse.

"SHE'S GOING TO BE DIFFICULT," Cal told Sum over lunch at a small restaurant near Killibrew Traders.

"Juniper's always difficult."

"The model executive, hmm?"

"She tries to be."

"And succeeds, from what I've seen."

Sum sighed. "Do you want me to talk to her?"

"No, she's my problem now."

"You won't tell her—"

"I won't tell her anything you've asked to keep between us, Sum. I don't pretend to understand a single one of you Killibrews, but I'm a man of my word."

Sum nodded, looking relieved. "I didn't mean to imply you weren't, Cal. I'm sorry about Juniper."

"Don't be." Cal raised his beer to his lips and thought of the gentle curve of Juniper Killibrew's mouth and the wiseass look in her eye. "She could prove to be one hell of a challenge. And you know me, Sum, I like a challenge."

Sum looked up at his friend in surprise but, prudently said nothing.

THAT EVENING Juniper was standing on her brand-new stepladder scraping wallpaper with her brand-new putty knife when Bo began running back and forth in the empty living room and wagging his tail. Worthless creature that he was, he was telling her in his own way that a visitor was at hand, or an intruder. It made no difference to him.

She climbed down off the stepladder. Even her sneakers landing on the hardwood floor echoed, but she was used to the sounds of emptiness and silence in the big old house. For her evening's work, she'd tied a batik scarf—page ninety of both the men's and women's catalogs—over her hair and put on jade rugby-weight sweatpants and sweatshirt, cover of the sport's catalog. Beethoven's Ninth Symphony was blaring on the stereo, the only piece of furniture in the adjoining dining room. That room, however, had a wall-to-wall carpet of a putrid shade of gold.

The symphony was in the fourth movement. One might as well have the illusion of class and chic, Juniper thought, singing along while peeling off layers of ugly, uglier and ugliest wallpaper and contemplating the poisoning of both her uncle and her new employer.

She was no longer feeling charitable toward Summerfield. He was a forty-year-old man, an adult, an educated individual in a position of responsibility; he'd let Calvin Gilliam use him and had himself behaved like an inconsiderate ass. Summerfield lacked the courage—the common decency—to tell her privately and in advance that he was selling out. Even after his announcement that morning, he hadn't bothered to come to her and explain. He'd snuck off—*slunk* off—like the snake in the grass he was.

Rumor had it he'd left town. She hoped so—for his sake.

"The lily liver," she muttered. Bo was jumping up and down. "Okay, okay, let's see who's out there."

She went to the front hall and peered out a leaded glass window, one of many in the sprawling house, and stood on tiptoe so she could see over the overgrown rhododendrons. Then the doorbell rang, more or less. It was really more of a wretched creak, the doorbell being one of the many, many things that needed fixing or replacement. She tugged open the solid walnut door. In a fit of Juniper didn't know what, the last tenants, a group of students, had painted the door bright orange. It clashed with the rhododendrons.

A middle-aged woman smiled at her from behind a long, white box tied with a blood-red bow. "Juniper Killibrew?"

"That's me."

"These are for you."

"Me?"

"I doubt there are two Juniper Killibrews in Portsmouth."

After the woman had left, Juniper opened the box with perfectly steady hands. Inside were a dozen long-stemmed roses. Pleased but suspicious, Juniper took them into the kitchen and laid them in the middle of her round oak table. They were gorgeous.

There was a card. She plucked it from the leaves and tore it open. It said, "Please stay. CG."

She didn't know whether to be offended, delighted, angry or amused. Just who did the man think he was dealing with? Did he honestly believe she could be bought off, pacified and mollified with a dozen roses?

The nerve of the man!

She called her friend the innkeeper and learned that Gilliam was again staying there. "Send up a bottle of your best whiskey," Juniper said. "Tell him pirates always get drunk after a pillage."

"Juniper, I couldn't . . ."

"Then write it on a card and pretend you don't know what it says."

"Shall I sign your name?"

"Just put 'JK.' He'll know."

Feeling very smug, Juniper put the roses in a big cut glass vase and returned to the last chords of Beethoven and her wallpaper.

Thirty minutes later Juniper was elbow deep in a
bucket of hot water, which was having no visible effect
on the tenacity of the first several layers of wallpaper,
and she was speckled with bits of paper and old paste.
Her entire front was soaked. Bo chose that moment to
go into his act again.

What next, she wondered, Swiss truffles?

No. It was Calvin Gilliam himself.

He was clean, dry and clad in his close-fitting jeans,
looking striking and unpredictable and, she had to admit, very sexy. He seemed surprised to see her in such
a soaked and disheveled state. But Juniper, never self-
conscious, merely scowled at him. "You're determined
to harass me, aren't you?" she demanded. "It's un-
professional!"

"Seems to me you're quite capable of responding in
kind."

She wondered if he'd drunk any of her whiskey. Too
much, perhaps? Somehow a dozen long-stemmed roses
hadn't drawn a measured, professional response from
her. She'd been impulsive, not her style, and yet she
hadn't thought to regret her action. Until now.

"Aren't you going to invite me in?" he asked.

"Why should I?"

He shrugged. "I want to talk."

"I don't. I'm still thinking."

His thick brows arched as he made a point of taking
in her dishevelment. Standing in the night air, she herself noticed that her nipples were outlined by the chilly,
wet fabric of her sweatshirt. She supposed he'd already noticed. To her regret, she realized her skin was
more sensitive, tingling almost, than it had been a few

minutes ago, with only Bo and the cats for company. The Killibrew curse on its women, she thought.

"One can think and scrape wallpaper at the same time," she pointed out. "Or at least I can."

"You look as if you could use a break."

"As a matter of fact, I was about to heat up some soup." She stood back from the door. "You might as well come in."

She led him through the main hall, past the sweeping curve of the front staircase, which would have been dramatic but for the nasty bottle-green shag carpeting on each and every step. And she didn't think there were any flowers as big, as ugly and as yellow anywhere in the world as those on her staircase wall.

Calvin Gilliam, millionaire rogue, surveyed the scene with frank distaste and followed her into the kitchen, which he eyed with equal disbelief. It was a bizarre combination of Victorian opulence—copper sink, high ceilings, walnut butler's pantry, acres of cabinets—and early ranch house—tacky wallpaper, crummy linoleum floor, Formica countertops. There was nothing cozy about it, and it was barely functional.

"I thought you were the condo-by-the-shore type," Calvin Gilliam remarked dryly.

"The place has potential," Juniper said.

Bo presented himself to Gilliam to be scratched. To Juniper's surprise, Gilliam obliged. "You live here alone?" he asked.

"Just me and the Summerfield ghosts. Have a seat. Would you care for some soup?"

"What kind?"

"White pea and a little this and that."

"Sounds ominous."

She shrugged. "It's a great way to keep stuff from moldering in the refrigerator."

"I think I'll pass."

That wasn't very nice of her, Juniper thought. She'd actually bought the soup at a posh deli in town but couldn't remember what it was called. Who had time to cook? And if Gilliam looked, he'd see there wasn't much beyond orange juice and a couple of dried-up limes in her refrigerator. She dumped the soup in a saucepan and dug out two bran muffins. They were a bit stale, but a few minutes in the toaster oven would freshen them up. She popped them in.

Belatedly she remembered to wash the glue off her hands.

"The roses offended you," Gilliam said. He'd been watching her bustle about the kitchen, but seemed unaware of the effect he was having on her damp, chilly and now somewhat aroused body.

"Not in and of themselves." She dried her hands with a paper towel. "They're quite lovely. But I'm a professional, Mr. Gilliam. I can't be wooed by flowers and chocolates."

"Chocolates?"

"Swiss truffles—my favorites. I thought you might send them next. Anyway, they won't work, either. And I dare say you wouldn't have sent me roses if I were a man."

He gently touched one of the bright blossoms and, impossibly, she found her gaze riveted to that single index finger, imagining it—

No, she wouldn't. Just because he couldn't act in a professional manner didn't mean she couldn't.

"The flowers," he said, "are only an indication of how desperate I am to have you stay with Traders."

"Horsefeathers."

He looked up at her sharply, and something in his eyes told her she was very right, indeed, to have called his bluff. There was nothing the least bit desperate about Calvin Gilliam. And now he knew she knew it.

"Aren't you loyal to the family name?" he asked.

"I'm sure you and I have radically different interpretations of loyalty, duty and success, Mr. Gilliam."

He grinned suddenly. "You can call me Cal, you know."

"I can call you a number of things," she muttered, turning to her soup.

"Pirate, for instance?"

She hadn't intended him to hear that last remark. "Perhaps." She grabbed a wooden spoon and stirred. *Why* had she let him in?

"You know, I might not let you resign. I might just go ahead and fire you."

"It's called 'outplaced' these days."

"Not by me. Believe me, you won't be 'outplaced,' Juniper. You'll be fired."

She laid down the wooden spoon. A strange heat was coursing through her, and it had nothing to do with anger or embarrassment. Calvin Gilliam wasn't your average sneaky bastard. She would have to be extremely careful, not only of him, but of herself. Her body was giving her fair warning.

"Do I detect a change in tactics, Mr. Gilliam?" she asked with a sly smile. "If I can't be sweet-talked, perhaps I can be threatened. Get the woman's dander up and see if she tells you to go to hell—or cowers and obeys."

"I have a feeling it will be neither."

"I asked you to give me some time to think."

"Juniper, I just want to be reasonable."

She lowered the heat under the soup and got out a bowl. "No, you don't," she said, turning to him. He was leaning back in the oak chair, watching her. "You want *me* to be reasonable. And you know that I have no grounds to be anything but very, difficult. You used my uncle, Mr. Gilliam. Now you propose to use me."

"Sum sold Killibrew Traders of his own free will," Calvin Gilliam said, his teeth only slightly clenched, but even that, Juniper reflected, was something. He was a man who was a natural at self-control, but Juniper supposed she did try his patience. It was a thought she relished. "Don't blame me for wanting to buy a profitable and exciting company," he went on. "In my position, you'd do the same."

"My wildest nightmares wouldn't put me in your position, Mr. Gilliam. You talked Summerfield into selling."

"Has he told you that?"

She buttered the two muffins and put them on plates. "I know my uncle."

"You'll have to take up the reasons he sold with him. As far as I'm concerned, what's done is done. All I want to do now is to make peace with you so we can ensure the transition of ownership without any major disruptions. I want you to stay on as vice president. Yes, my reasons are selfish—you're just good. Look, nothing needs to change. You can continue working with a free rein. I'll stay the hell out of your way."

"If today's any indication—"

"Damn it, today's just an indication of how *reasonable* I intend to be—and how much I want you."

She nearly dropped the muffins.

"As vice president," he added quickly, but there was a huskiness to his voice that she found troubling. "Juniper, why upset your life? You have a good job, your house here, your friends—do you want to give that up just to get back at me for taking advantage of a business opportunity?"

She sat across from him with her bowl of soup and pushed a plate with a muffin on it over to him. "What makes you so sure I'll quit?"

His gaze was direct and honest, surprising her. "Because in your position, I would." He rose suddenly and stood very close to her, so that she could both see the muscles in his arms and the flatness of his stomach and feel her own muscles, very low in her body, responding. "Have a good dinner, Ms Killibrew. I apologize for the roses."

She managed a smile. "I'll enjoy them anyway. I'll pretend they were sent by a secret lover."

He smiled, an unexpected gleam of amusement in his eyes; a twinkle, she thought. "Perhaps they were."

He offered to see himself out and departed, a detectable jauntiness to his step.

Well, Juniper thought, hadn't she set herself up for that one?

BACK IN HIS ROOM at the inn, Cal lay on the quilted coverlet of the four-poster bed and consumed more than he should have of Juniper's bottle of whiskey. Juniper Killibrew. A hell of a name. A hell of a woman, too. Prickly and poisonous, Sum had said. How true, how true. But interesting . . . compelling, lively, smart. The "normal" one of the Killibrew family, Summerfield had also indicated, if there could be such a thing. *Not* Cal's type. She was reliable, hardworking, proper, starchy.

And she had haunting gray eyes and a pert, sexy little body that could drive him wild.

"Good Lord, man," he muttered to himself, "she's a by-the-book exec."

Nevertheless, he couldn't seem to get her out of his mind. And he felt this nagging guilt; it made him downright uncomfortable. He'd stolen the Killibrew legacy from that cool, gray-eyed, tantalizing individual. Or he felt as if he had. But dammit, why should he? It was her own father who'd sold off his Killibrew Traders stock to his younger brother. Cal had had nothing to do with that.

Yet he had to admit that if he hadn't agreed to buy Killibrew Traders, hadn't encouraged Sum in his scheme, Sum probably never would have gotten his act together enough to offer the company elsewhere. Cal had been there, handy and greedy—and also determined, he reminded himself, to help his friend realize a long-cherished dream. A good dream. Perhaps even a noble one.

Of course, Juniper Killibrew wouldn't see it that way. She was too damned proper. A stodgy Yankee. An M.B.A. type.

Who lived in a rambling wreck of a Victorian house with a bright orange door. Whom he wanted to escort up her ugly stairs to whatever she used as a bedroom and make passionate love to.

Cal simply didn't know what to make of any of it. The orange door. The house. The dog. The cats. The soup and stale muffins. Juniper Killibrew herself and how ridiculously much he wanted her.

He poured himself another glass of whiskey. Business was business, he told himself. If Juniper quit, she quit. He'd find someone to take her place and get on with it.

But who, he wondered, could replace a woman like that?

4

JUNIPER DRESSED in pale-yellow linen and dragged herself to her office the next morning, arriving at her usual seven-thirty. At nine, when Beth came in, Juniper asked if Summerfield had shown up. Not to her surprise, he hadn't. She asked if Calvin Gilliam was in. Again not to her surprise, he wasn't. Killibrew Traders was being left up to her. As usual. Peas from the same bad pod, Summerfield and Gilliam were counting on her sense of duty and loyalty to persuade her to continue as before, working her tail off, never complaining, always making a profit.

They were counting wrong. Arms crossed, she paced in front of her desk. She couldn't change what was. Summerfield had sold Killibrew Traders, and there wasn't a thing she could do about it—except annoy the hell out of the new owner. "Do anything, Juniper," Summerfield had once told her, "but don't quit. Killibrew Traders wouldn't last a month without you."

She knew better than to believe that. But that wasn't the point. The point was Summerfield believed it. And if he did, presumably so did Calvin Gilliam, at least to some degree. Neither wanted her to leave Killibrew Traders. If nothing else, they knew a good thing when they saw one, especially when it meant they didn't have to roll up their sleeves and go to work.

Well, so be it. The only thing to do was quit.

She sagged against a file cabinet and looked around her office. Leave all this? Was revenge worth it? Would she just be cutting off her nose to spite her face?

Beth poked her head through the door. "Cable for you, Juniper."

Her parents! Maybe her family would help her out—not that they ever had before, but never before had Killibrew Traders been sold to an outsider. Juniper wondered if this once they might rally round her.

But naturally not. "Sum must follow his own path," the cable said, in her father's words. "So must you. Why not come to Tonga? Kisses, Mum and Dad."

Useless. She sighed and sat in her high-backed leather swivel chair. Perhaps, she thought, if she'd gone into medicine, following the straight and narrow path of her mother instead of the winding, treacherous road of the Killibrews, she wouldn't be facing this predicament. She could be doing good in the world. Commerce was such a nasty business.

She pivoted to look out the window. It was a clear, warm day, summerlike. But I *am* doing good, she thought stubbornly. She wasn't a sleazeball executive. She ran a profitable company, not only for her own benefit and that of her shiftless uncle, but also for the benefit of the employees, who received fair wages and benefits and worked in decent conditions. Morale was high at Killibrew Traders. Management-employee relations were a model for other similar, medium-size companies. It wasn't saving lives, but it was something. And she was proud of her work.

So? It could be done elsewhere. Her contributions to Killibrew Traders were over. Period. *Fini.*

She called her sister in Colorado, at a lodge, getting her out of bed. She was between camps and treating herself to some spring skiing. "Hey, June!" Even just awakened, Sage sounded fit and ebullient and well in control of her life, as always. "How's the sweat house?"

It had been Sage's fondest dream since childhood never to work a single second at the family firm. Thus far, she hadn't. Juniper said without preamble, "Summerfield sold out to a corporate raider."

"Who?"

"Calvin Gilliam."

"Don't know him."

Of course not. Sage didn't read the *Wall Street Journal.* Juniper explained.

"Well, June," Sage said, "I guess you should have bought Traders stock when you had the chance, instead of that drafty old house, huh?"

Juniper said nothing. Leave it to Sage to turn the whole business around and blame it on the one time her older sister had acted on impulse instead of reason. Two years before Summerfield would have been glad to have sold Traders stock to Juniper—and at a reasonable price. But Summerfield House, such as it was, had gone on the market. With the burgeoning popularity of Victorians, it didn't exactly go for a song, either. So much for Juniper's savings. But as far as she'd been concerned, it had been do or die with the house. With Killibrew Traders, there was always a tomorrow.

Until today.

"June?"

"I'm here."

"This Gilliam character doesn't want to fire you, does he?"

"No, quite the contrary. He's anxious to have me stay."

Sage breathed in obvious relief. "Well, then there's no problem. Hey, it was nice talking to you—"

"No problem! Sage—Sage, I'm the last of the Killibrews of Killibrew Traders!"

"So? Enjoy." And she hung up.

"Sisters," Juniper muttered, grabbing her handbag from the centerfold of last winter's catalog.

She headed outside. The crab apples flanking the parking lot were in full bloom, but the fresh air and beauty of the surroundings only depressed her. Her family had never been any help before. Why should they be now? Damn Summerfield. Damn Calvin Gilliam for taking advantage of him. For sending her roses. For having pale-cornflower eyes and being different and appealing and therefore dangerous.

There. If she stayed ornery, she thought, she might not have to be reasonable.

She climbed into her vintage mustard-colored Volvo and just sat there for a few minutes. She felt like driving away—anywhere—it didn't matter. Concord, Boston, Maine, Canada, Michigan. What difference did it make? She had a full tank of gas, a wallet full of credit cards. She could just go. The hell with the house, the job, the feckless uncle, the callous family, the handsome pirate.

Of course, there was Bo to consider, and the cats. She couldn't just go off and leave them, could she?

"You have friends who'd feed them," she told herself aloud.

True, she thought, starting up the car. But then she'd have to come back. When she left, she wanted to be gone for good.

Right now she'd settle for a visit to the waterfront condominium of one Summerfield Killibrew.

CAL HAD AWAKENED with a headache and now, sitting alone in the inn's sunlit breakfast room, he had no desire to be pleasant to an old woman. He hoped the one marching toward him would keep right on marching and drop her bony old frame at someone else's table. But he didn't think she would. There was something distinctly Killibrew about her. She had that devil-may-care look that he'd seen in Sum and his difficult niece. And the eyes. They were giant and round and a hauntingly clear gray. Sum didn't have them. But Juniper did.

Without asking, the elderly woman pulled out the chair opposite him and sat down. She had removed a floppy straw hat, which she now laid in her lap, and then tucked a few stray curls back among her many bobby pins. But there were too many stray curls and not nearly enough bobby pins. Her dress was deep tan linen, crisp, though ancient, and a perfect fit.

She smiled, and her worn face filled with the vibrancy and experience of a life lived well. "May I join you?"

There was a twinkle in her eyes, as if she knew full well that a robust young man such as Cal couldn't refuse an old woman such as herself a seat at his table. It was a nice ploy. She *had* to be a Killibrew, he thought, laying down his *Wall Street Journal*. "Certainly, Mrs. . . . ."

"Killibrew," she said. "Ms Killibrew."

She was not about to be patronized. He smiled. "How do you do. I'm—"

"Calvin Gilliam." She might have been saying "Attila the Hun."

"Cal," he said.

Her steely eyes narrowed, and he guessed he'd done something, said something that had confirmed an unpleasant preconception Ms Killibrew had about him. He wasn't sure what her preconception was, or what he'd said or done. He did know he didn't give a merry damn. After last night, he had concluded that the wisest, simplest, least painful course of action would be for him to depart from the sedate streets of Portsmouth, New Hampshire, come morning. The Killibrews could sort matters out among themselves.

Obviously he hadn't made his discreet exit soon enough.

"I'm Summerfield and Juniper's aunt," she said. "Summerfield's aunt, Juniper's great-aunt, to be accurate."

Cal suspected Ms Killibrew would always insist upon being accurate.

"I've heard about you, Mr. Gilliam."

He poured himself coffee from a silver pot and gestured toward her, but she shook her head. He said, "About the sale of Killibrew Traders, you mean?"

"No. About *you.*"

"I see." There was something about her knowing, sanctimonious look that prodded him to ask what, under ordinary circumstances, he never would have asked. "What have you heard, Ms Killibrew?"

She squared her shoulders. "That you're an incomparable rogue."

He nearly spat coffee. "I beg your pardon?"

"Unscrupulous," she said. "Merciless. Alert to a good deal and a soft touch." Her eyes narrowed. "Arrogant."

Cal wondered if he should be shocked. Had Juniper filled her great-aunt with these—well, he couldn't exactly call them lies—these exaggerations? "Did you come here to insult me?" he asked mildly.

"No, indeed not." She seemed horrified. "I'm merely repeating what I've heard."

Yes, from Juniper. "Why?"

"Because I feel I must warn you."

"Warn me?" The woman had to be in her late seventies at least, but nothing in her demeanor suggested she expected to be underestimated. Cal had no intention of doing so. Sum had surprised him. Juniper had surprised him. Why shouldn't their old aunt surprise him? "Warn me about what?" he repeated.

"About me."

In a single, regal sweep she was on her feet, hat and archaic purse in hand. "I'll be watching you, Mr. Gilliam," she went on. "If you do anything that suggests to me you've taken advantage of my nephew or my great-niece, you will have to contend with *me*."

Cal just stared.

"Am I making myself clear?"

He could see she wasn't going to leave without an answer. "You are," he said.

"Good."

And she marched off. Cal ordered a fresh pot of coffee and wondered, not for the first time, if buying Killibrew Traders was among the dumber things he'd done in his life. And, he asked himself with a wry smile, conjuring up images of Juniper, precisely what did this elderly Killibrew mean by "taking advantage of"?

SUMMERFIELD HESITANTLY opened the door of his seaside condominium, located on the second floor of a converted bleached-shingle house. He tried to shut the door in Juniper's face, but she had already angled her foot in the way, and he backed off. Worthless as a businessman, in his niece's opinion, Summerfield was nonetheless a kind enough man. Breaking Juniper's foot *and* shattering her life all in one week would have been too much for him.

Retreating slightly, he ran a hand through his wild tawny hair. "Juniper, what a surprise. How are you?"

He even smiled, which only infuriated her more. Glaring at him, she followed him into the spacious, sunlit condo. Long windows overlooked the ocean, blue-green and glistening in the midmorning sun.

"I'd heard you'd fled," she said. "Bit late with your escape, aren't you?"

"Juniper—"

"You know Killibrews: they never like to face the victims of their irresponsibility and underhandedness."

Looking pained, her uncle seated himself on the very edge of a sectional sofa. He was wearing casual separates from the sport catalog and already had a light golden tan. In his own way he was a good-looking rascal, but Juniper had to admit she'd never paid much attention to Summerfield as a person, merely as a professional, an incompetent one, at that. But perhaps she was being hard on him. He'd been married once ages ago and had his share of flings, but at forty he'd made no apparent moves to establish himself in anything, certainly not in marriage or business. He was a man of whims.

"You shouldn't talk," he said. "You're one of us, you know."

"A white sheep in a family of black sheep."

He nodded, looking miserable if not entirely guilt-ridden, and Juniper felt herself softening toward him. Blaming Summerfield for the results of his disastrous friendship with Calvin Gilliam was like blaming a flounder for being swallowed up by a shark. If only he'd come to her first! *She* could have handled Gilliam.

Sighing, she eased herself onto a chair and felt weariness overcome her. It was more than just physical fatigue. She was tired of it all, of working so damned hard and killing herself trying to fight family tradition. Why bother? Why not just be like them? Sell off the house, buy a boat and sail around the world, without telling anyone, of course.

"Can I get you anything?"

She eyed him. "I could shoot you, Summerfield. You know that?"

"Juniper—it can't be that bad," he said reasonably. "What's the difference, working for one absentee president or another? Cal won't stand in your way—"

"Summerfield, you're a *Killibrew*."

He blinked at her in confusion. "I thought you considered that a fault, not a virtue."

"It's a simple fact. Oh, you'll never understand, will you? I'm the last of the Killibrews at Killibrew Traders." It had become her refrain. "I have no power—"

"No power?" He looked shocked. "Juniper, you have the only power that counts: you can make or break the company."

"Every executive is replaceable. The second I begin to think otherwise, I'm doomed. And don't think that's something Gilliam doesn't know."

"Has he threatened to fire you?"

She shrugged. "In a roundabout sort of way."

"You mean he'll fire you before he'll let you quit. Juniper—Juniper, maybe I should warn you about him."

"A little late, don't you think?"

"We're good friends—I'd trust him with my life—but he's not me. He doesn't have my patience. He doesn't know you the way I do, appreciate your eccentricities—"

"My *what*!"

"Well, you know."

"No, I don't."

"Look, all I'm saying is Cal might not be as willing to put up with your . . . well, your intractability."

She frowned at her uncle. "Are you saying I'm a pain in the ass, Summerfield?"

He smiled. "We all have our moments."

She decided to leave it at that. Obviously Summerfield didn't know her well at all. "So what are you going to do with the money?"

He jumped up and turned his back to her, staring out toward the ocean, stuffing his hands in his pockets and looking profoundly uncomfortable. "I didn't do this for profit. I've always had enough money to live. You know that."

"Then *why*, Summerfield?"

"I wanted out."

"Not good enough."

He glanced sideways at her. "Isn't it?"

She supposed he had a point. It had been good enough reason for her father and her grandfather to bail out. Their hearts hadn't been in clothes. Simple. And a dangerous precedent. "You're going to blow the money, aren't you?"

"Juniper—"

"What are you going to do? Finance a dogsled trip to the North Pole? Explore the Himalayas? Backpack through Africa? You know, uncle, there are hundreds— thousands—of ways a Killibrew can dispose of large sums of money." She rose and clapped him on the shoulder in a sarcastic gesture of camaraderie. "Just try not to blow it all in one day, okay?"

He gave her a serious look, the patience he'd bragged about in short supply. "Get off your moral high horse, Juniper Killibrew," he told her quietly. "You've precious little room to talk. Who the hell sank all her money into that monstrosity of a house?"

"A family treasure, not something I'd expect you of all people to understand! I believe in tradition—I care about this family."

"So do I!"

His intensity surprised her, but she didn't back off. "Not about me, you don't."

He looked stricken. "Juniper, my God . . ."

"Save it, Summerfield. And remember: at least I've *earned* my money."

It was a nasty parting shot, and she stormed out, leaving him standing speechless before his view of the ocean. Tears of anger and frustration stung her eyes, but she refused to cry. And true to his Killibrew nature, her uncle didn't come out to try to stop her and talk, explain, apologize, even yell. He could have blamed everything on his "friend," Calvin Gilliam. Juniper had Cal's roses in the middle of her kitchen table; she'd have understood.

When Juniper returned to her office, she sat staring out across the sprawling lawns of Killibrew Traders for a very long time, thinking. But nothing changed. Nothing would. She could see that now. There were no choices left.

She buzzed Beth. "I'd like you to take a memo, please."

But once Beth was sitting in front of Juniper's desk with a steno pad, Juniper saw the look of pain and concern and guessed her secretary knew what was coming. Juniper wondered if she were being as irresponsible as her uncle. Was she making her own escape now? It didn't matter. The decision was made. And it was irrevocable.

"It's to Calvin Gilliam," she said. "Have it delivered by messenger, if you would. Begin Dear Mr. Gilliam—" She heaved a sigh and stopped. "No, never mind. Take a break, Beth, and let me use your typewriter. I'll deal with this myself."

"What is it?" Beth asked, not that she hadn't already guessed.

Juniper looked grim. "It's a letter of resignation."

CAL DIDN'T RECEIVE Juniper's letter until he returned to the inn that evening. He'd decided to stick around Portsmouth for a while—but to steer clear of Killibrews. He'd spent the day alone, sailing, thinking and staying away from his new company and its vice president of marketing and sales. He didn't want to influence Juniper's decision, unless, of course, he could be assured the results would be to his advantage. Instead he had the uncomfortable feeling his presence would only serve to remind Juniper of just what she was getting herself into.

He wondered if old Ms Killibrew had told her greatniece about their meeting. Probably bragged about calling him an unscrupulous, merciless and an arrogant rogue. He laughed. He couldn't help it. A rogue, for heaven's sake. And an incomparable one at that.

But he didn't want Juniper to leave Killibrew Traders. He knew that much. It wasn't a question of being nice, he told himself. It was just good business. If she left he would have to find someone to replace her, which would require a considerable expenditure of effort on his part. Or even more unpleasant, he'd have to step in himself. Juniper Killibrew was accustomed to doing the work of three people, even thrived on it, if he knew the type. But not Cal Gilliam. That was why he owned companies and pretty much left the running of them to the ranks of his trusted associates, under his watchful eye, of course.

Juniper, he reminded himself, was hardly a trusted associate. She was a woman who played by the rules . . . except for her orange door. A definite problem, that orange door was. It didn't fit with the rest of her dignified self.

Or did it?

He asked himself, *Who the devil cares?*

Not for the first time that day, he wondered if he simply didn't want Juniper Killibrew to march herself angrily out of his life. Did he want her because it was good business, or because he was intrigued by the contradictions and the bridled passion of her?

The innkeeper handed him the letter, in a brown-on-buff Killibrew Traders business envelope, very regal, but he didn't open it until he'd reached his room and poured himself a glass of sherry.

The letter was neatly typed.

Dear Mr. Gilliam:
This letter is to inform you of my decision, effective immediately, to resign my position with Killibrew Traders. I congratulate you on your recent purchase and look forward to the continued success of the company. Please do not try to contact me regarding this irrevocable decision. I shall be leaving New Hampshire forthwith to begin compiling my memoirs.

Sincerely,
Juniper Killibrew

Cal balled the thing up and tossed it in the trash. But there was no satisfaction in that. He snatched it from the wastebasket, tore the one hundred percent cotton rag into bits, dumped them in an ashtray and lit the mess with a wooden match. He watched until it burned to ashes.

He didn't feel better.

"'Forthwith,'" he raved. "Who the devil uses words like 'forthwith'?"

On his way down the narrow, early-nineteenth-century stairs of the elegant inn, he resisted pounding the walls with the two powerful fists he'd made and couldn't seem to unmake.

"'Memoirs,'" he muttered through clenched teeth, seething. So much for his renowned sense of calm. "'Memoirs!'"

If Juniper Killibrew didn't watch herself, he'd damn well see to it that her memoirs were published posthumously!

JUNIPER HAD TOSSED OUT the dried-up limes and drunk the orange juice in her refrigerator, called the post office to stop delivery of her mail and arranged to have a teenage girl down the street mow the lawn as necessary, which undoubtedly would be more often than Juniper herself mowed it. She'd wrapped her roses in wet newspaper and aluminum foil. It wasn't their fault that they'd been sent by a rogue, and they were beautiful.

She did feel a momentary pang of guilt at leaving her wallpaper in such an unfinished state, but what the hell, she thought, it would be there when she came back, just as unfinished. Or the next owner could deal with it if she didn't come back.

Her heart jumped. Good heavens! Was it possible she wasn't coming back?

"Yes, of course it is," she said aloud. "You knew that when you typed your letter of resignation."

She felt no satisfaction in having quit. The revenge wasn't sweet at all. There was no exhilaration, no sense of euphoria at having stuck it to Calvin Gilliam—only a sense of loss. Not only loss of job, but of friends. Of community. Of family tradition.

Well, she was only thirty-one, she told herself stoutly. She'd start over somewhere else.

Perhaps she would have felt better if she'd been around to see Gilliam read her letter. Only moments ago her innkeeper friend had called to say Gilliam's stomping had loosened the plaster on the ceiling.

There was a silver lining in every cloud, Juniper decided with rekindled amusement.

"Hello . . ."

The voice, deep and male and very liquid, came from the front porch. Juniper had left the orange door open so the sunlight and breeze could come through the screen.

Gilliam. She dropped her arms to her side in a huff but remained in the living room. Maybe if she left him alone he'd just go away, like a hornet.

"Juniper," he said tightly, "I know you're here."

Of course he did. Her door was open, her car was out front and Bo and the cats were sniffing at the screens.

"I want to talk."

Now he sounded perfectly sane and reasonable, not as if he'd stomped plaster into the innkeeper's soup pot. But just too bad. There was nothing to talk about. She picked up a plastic bucket of water, vinegar, soap and old wallpaper paste, unemptied from last night, and headed around to the front door.

Dark-haired and as unrepentantly sexy as ever, Calvin Gilliam was peering through the screen door. He scowled when he saw her. With her bucket of slimy water, her Killibrew Traders sweatshirt and her elastic-waist pants, relics from a mid-seventies Killibrew Traders catalog, Juniper supposed she didn't look especially businesslike or intimidating, and hardly alluring. He probably thought she looked like a hag. She hoped so. There was no point in bringing sex into all this.

But she knew that was hopeless. Sex had been involved from the beginning.

"Go away," she said.

He stood back from the screen. "Why?"

"Because if you don't, I'll throw this bucket of water at you."

"Is it clean?"

"No."

"What's in it?"

"Old wallpaper paste. Soap. Vinegar. It smells."

"Then I suggest you march quietly somewhere and dump it."

She stared at him. "You do, do you?"

"I do. Before *I* dump it on *you*."

She snorted. "That I'd love to see!"

He placed a hand high on the doorframe and bent one knee, looking very cocky. It was almost worth heaving the bucket of slosh right through the screen at him, just to destroy the effect. Of course, Juniper reasoned, that would be childish. And there would be the mess to mop up afterward. Also him to deal with. He was the sort of man who would relish appropriate revenge. She had to suppress a vision of him hauling her up her green-carpeted stairs.

"If you'll stand aside," she said haughtily, but a bit breathlessly, "I'll toss it off the side of the porch."

He looked dubious. "Will the stuff kill anything?"

"No, but if you'll look, there's nothing living on the other end of the porch."

He glanced to his left. *Now*, she thought, and her fingers itched on the bucket. She could drench him and run like hell.

But she resisted. A future employer, she told herself, might wish to discuss her with Calvin Gilliam, and he might just mention he'd been doused with a bucketful of slimy water when things hadn't gone her way.

He moved away from the door. She walked out onto the porch and dumped the bucket over the side. It really did stink. But her actions were very mature, she decided. Very reasonable—and not at all satisfying.

Swinging the bucket, she about-faced.

Gilliam was now leaning against the wide rail along the front of the big Victorian porch. He nodded to her. "Where are you going?"

"Back inside."

His face darkened. She knew he'd meant where was she going in her car, which was half-packed, but she'd deliberately chosen to be obtuse, of which he was extremely well aware.

"In the car," he said stiffly. "I noticed you're packing."

She shrugged. "I'm leaving town."

"Why?"

His directness was intriguing, a quality she admired in people, but also disturbing. He seemed to be probing her soul. She looked away. "It's the Killibrew thing to do."

"Juniper, dammit!"

She heard his sigh, more distressed than annoyed, compelling her to turn around. He had crossed his arms over his chest. He was in handsome, pleated khakis today and a pastel safari shirt, both too stylish for the classic pages of a Killibrew Traders men's catalog. The company he'd just purchased believed in clothes that could be worn forever. Clearly, its new owner didn't.

"Juniper," he said more calmly, "I got your letter, and I think you're being rash. Look—I've given your situation some thought. I didn't want to make any changes myself in the company, at least not right away—"

"Why not?" She feigned indifference. "It's your company."

"I'm majority stockholder," he said, his eyes cool. "That's all."

"As I said, your company."

"I'm not a dictator, contrary to whatever slander you may have heard about me." He inhaled deeply, controlling himself, she realized. She supposed she could be extremely annoying when she felt like it. Right now she felt like it. "Juniper," he went on, "I'm well aware you've been doing your work *and* Sum's. Suppose we change that."

"Go ahead. Bring in a real president and CEO. It makes no difference to me."

"It would." His eyes held hers. "Because you're the person I have in mind."

"Ah."

He looked surprised at her casual response; it wasn't what he'd been expecting. "I'm thinking of a seventy-five percent increase in salary."

"Why not double it?" she suggested carelessly.

"All right. Doubled."

Her spine stiffened. "After all, you can afford it," she said. Swinging her bucket at her side, she waltzed inside, but stopped to look at him through the screen. "You're missing the point, Mr. Gilliam. I have integrity. I can't be flattered, and I can't be bought."

"And I can't help it," he snapped back in a low, deadly voice, "if your uncle wanted to sell and I had the money to buy."

"Poor, poor Cal." She was being very sarcastic.

As he leaped to his feet, she shut her orange door and left him there seething on her porch.

But he was even more determined than she'd anticipated; he came around the back and walked right into her kitchen, where she was shoving the bucket under the sink. Suddenly she wished she hadn't been reasonable and had thrown the whole stinking mess at him. Clearly he didn't bring out the qualities on which she prided herself. She— Well, she was reminding herself of Grandpa Killibrew. "You don't give up, do you," she said, not making it a question.

"Not easily." He remained in the doorway, and she saw how straight-backed and tense and irritated he was. And yet those spectacular eyes of his were focused on her in a way she found distinctly unsettling. "Juniper, can't we be partners?"

The words were conciliatory. Except for the eyes, which were unreadable, everything else—the tone in which he spoke, the expression, the pose—was decidedly not conciliatory. She had the feeling Calvin Gilliam would get more satisfaction out of throwing slimy water at *her*. Perhaps they had something in common, after all.

She didn't even hesitate. "No, we can't."

"Dammit—"

"Last night you threatened to fire me. How could we be partners?"

"Idle talk."

"It doesn't matter. We can't be partners, because you have financial power and I don't. You're in a position to fire me. I'm not in a position to fire you."

"Only to harass me," he muttered, beside himself.

She sniffed. "I've acted like a professional."

He pounded a fist on her counter, just once, but didn't take a step toward her. She spotted a can of bug killer under the sink. Would it work? There was a fly-swatter, too. And carpet deodorizer and cleanser. A whole arsenal of weapons. She decided not to stand up.

"A professional," he was saying, very nearly shouting, "would recognize the enormous power you *do* have! It's you—Juniper Killibrew—who makes or breaks Killibrew Traders, not me. Partners don't have to be identical to be equals. We can have different sources of strength and power."

She said coolly, "Not in this case."

He groaned, ran a hand through his tousled hair, then threw up both hands in defeat. And looked at her with those strangely warm, pale eyes of his. "You're stubborn, aren't you?"

She smiled up at him. "Decisive."

"At least give me a month." He wasn't shouting now.

But Juniper wasn't fooled. "So you don't have to work? Forget it."

"It's the professional thing to do," he said slyly. "Help with the transition, give me some time to find a replacement. Any reasonable executive in your position would agree to that much."

"I suppose you have a point."

She could see him holding back a grin. "Then you'll do it? You'll give me a month?"

She shook her head. "I'll consider giving you a month."

As she'd expected, he didn't push his luck but promised to call her first thing in the morning, and retreated. She noticed the thrill of victory in his eyes and the bounce in his step as he shot through her back door.

But she had made a promise. She did consider giving him a month—and promptly rejected the idea. In a month Calvin Gilliam and his strong legs and blue eyes could probably persuade her to do anything at all. He was one very resourceful man.

For the first time, she wondered if her abrupt departure from Killibrew Traders had less to do with being the last of the Killibrews and all that sentimental blather than it did with the new owner himself. Not as owner, not as corporate pirate, not as friend of shiftless uncle who had betrayed her, but as himself. A man as stubborn as she was, as resourceful, as tenacious, as direct. He wasn't walking around on eggshells now; he wasn't afraid of her. He was challenging her head-on—and he had every intention of winning.

Or he wanted her to believe that was what he was doing. Muttering to herself, Juniper trudged upstairs. Given his treacherous nature, Gilliam could easily be following a careful plan to get her to remain at Killibrew Traders, not because he couldn't do without her, but because it was more convenient for him if he didn't have to.

And all her questions and doubts clearly meant she didn't trust him. Couldn't. Wouldn't. And, of course, *that* meant she had to go.

Now, she thought. Tonight.

5

CAL ASSUMED he'd won, and he arrived at Killibrew Traders on Wednesday with a spring in his step and a happy tune in his head. By buying Killibrew Traders he was more than helping out a friend, Cal saw that now. It was a chance, too, to work with a lively and intelligent woman. They'd be partners. He'd learn from her; she'd learn from him. *Damn*, he thought as he whistled his way down the corridor to the office of the vice president of marketing, *everything is going to work out just fine.*

Juniper's secretary, Beth, was sighing mournfully over her typewriter, but Cal refused to take this as a hint. He walked up to her desk. "I'd like to see Ms Killibrew, please."

"I'm sorry. Juniper's not in."

"What do you mean she's not in? It's past ten o'clock. I thought she was the efficient type."

"Oh, she is. But she's not here today."

"She sick?"

"No—"

"Then where the hell is she?"

Beth looked surprised. "I assumed you knew, Mr. Gilliam."

"Cal," he corrected automatically, but he could feel worry, and a touch of anger, prickling at the small of his back. "Assumed I knew what, Beth?"

"Well, that—Juniper cleaned out her desk yesterday. She's, er, left the company."

Feeling his heart thud heavily in his chest, Cal straightened. "But she changed her mind, didn't she tell you?"

"I really don't think so."

"You mean she's gone?"

"Yes, I do."

"Damn the woman!"

He stormed into her office. Spotless. Nary a pencil in sight. The miserable woman had been playing games with him. She'd never for a single second intended to give him so much as another hour of her time. She'd agreed to consider being reasonable just to—to what?

To get rid of him. Yes. That was it. He made her just as oddly uncomfortable as she made him. She had known he'd done everything in his power to stop himself from hauling her up by her elbows and kissing her until they were both senseless. She'd wanted it as much as he had but, for the sake of the company, out of some archaic sense of duty, he'd resisted, tried to remain professional, even impersonal. Hell of a lot of good it had done—something he would damn well remember in the future.

He stormed back to the outer office and glared at Beth, but quickly reminded himself it wasn't her fault that Juniper Killibrew was a liar and a sneak. He said tightly but with control, "Call her, please."

"Of course." With a steady hand Beth picked up her phone and pressed a button that automatically dialed what Cal presumed was Juniper's home number. There was an interminable wait, during which Beth didn't meet his eye. Then she hung up and glanced at him. "No answer, I'm afraid."

He swore under his breath but managed to smile and thank her before he left.

Cutting through the woods adjoining Killibrew Traders, he marched over to the rambling Victorian house. This time there was no mustard-colored Volvo standing in the cobblestone driveway, no dog and cats at the screens, no beautiful ash-blond woman threatening to throw a bucket of slimy water at him.

The orange door was locked up tight.

Juniper Killibrew was gone.

Feeling a peculiar mix of betrayal, anger and loss, Cal walked slowly back to Killibrew Traders and slipped unnoticed into the small corner office he'd decided to take over. He didn't feel right using Sum's office, because he wasn't a Killibrew, he supposed, although he'd had no such compunction with other companies. This one was different. He'd known that from the beginning. Power and money weren't so much issues here as family. People. He wasn't sure he liked that. From the very beginning he'd had his doubts about getting involved with the Killibrews.

Dammit, he thought with sudden vehemence, he should just cut his losses now. Objectively, he knew that. Juniper had made her decision to leave and acted on it, and there was nothing positive to be gained from pursuing her when she didn't want to be pursued. It wasn't ethical. And, he had to admit, she had done nothing he himself wouldn't have done in a similar position—except resist the impulse to dump the bucket over his head. He wouldn't have been able to do that.

He thought of her as she'd been last night. Righteously indignant, her wet breasts outlined against her soaked shirt. It was a troubling image. She'd looked like hell, and yet he'd never desired a woman as much as he'd desired her right then. He couldn't figure it out. He had to remind himself theirs was a business relationship—and, above all, Juniper Killibrew wasn't his sort of woman. He could almost hear his mother: "She's lovely. So responsible, so bright."

Yes, she was. And definitely not for him. He liked bright and intelligent women, but not ones who were so responsible they could never have any fun. What he felt for her was just . . . hormonal or something. Nothing to do with his brain, with logic.

He picked up the phone and called a number in New York. "Arthur? It's Cal. I need a favor." Arthur Green, Cal knew, owed him, and dearly. He was an M.B.A. type, as good as Juniper Killibrew at the corporate game, maybe better. He knew all the rules, broke them when he had to, played by them when he could. "I've got a catalog company here," Cal went on. "High quality, profitable. Need someone to mind shop a bit."

"How long?" Arthur asked.

"Indefinitely."

"I can give you three months."

Twelve weeks, ninety days . . . it might as well have been just an hour. But Cal was running short of options. "How soon can you get here?"

"Monday morning."

"Fine. I'll have reports sent to you."

"Cal . . . the name of the company?"

Cal laughed. Good old reliable Arthur. "Killibrew Traders."

Arthur grunted in satisfaction. "A good one. I'll see you Monday."

"Maybe, maybe not."

"Cal?"

"I could be in hot pursuit of your replacement—and predecessor."

"FIND HER," Cal said. "Find her and tell her."

Summerfield shook his head over his lunch plate. "It wouldn't do any good for me to try to explain anything now. First, she wouldn't listen. She doesn't *want* me to have a decent motive for selling. She wants me to be the 'feckless' uncle she assumes I've always been. Second, I can't have her interfering right now. It would be disastrous."

Cal frowned, in no mood for Sum's rationalizations. "Who the hell says she'd interfere?"

"It's her nature, Cal."

Simply put, Cal thought, and inarguable.

"This Arthur Green's the best," Sum went on. "Why not let him take over? To hell with Juniper."

"Artie can give me three months and trusts me not to try to twist his arm to do something he has no intention of doing, like extending his stay. Moving heaven and earth wouldn't faze him; come fall, his butt's back in New York. And besides, you don't mean 'to hell with Juniper.' You know she belongs here as well as I do."

Sum sighed, shaking his head in guilt and confusion. "I never thought she'd react like this. Never. It's just not like her, Cal. I knew she could be a problem, but quitting, running off— Hell, I just didn't expect it."

"Does it change anything, Sum? Any regrets?"

His friend didn't even hesitate. "Frankly, no. Juniper has a right to be pissed, but she's carrying this too far, in my opinion. No, Cal, no regrets."

"Any idea where she might be?"

Sum laughed. "You've got to be kidding. You think she told me, the feckless uncle?"

"Better than the scandalous new owner," Cal said dryly.

"Hmm. No, I haven't a clue, but— Wait a minute." He fished out a dime. "I've got a sweet old aunt who knows everything."

Cal made no comment. "Sweet" was not a word he would have chosen to describe the starchy old bird who'd warned him off. Perhaps there was another aunt. He shuddered at the very idea. At this point he'd met his full quota of Killibrews.

Sum put a call through at a pay phone and returned, grinning.

"Victory?" Cal asked.

"You bet. She's alone, she's isolated—and if you want her, Cal, she's all yours."

Cal gave him a look. "We are talking about Juniper, not this infamous aunt of yours."

"Indeed."

Leaning back and tracing a finger along the rim of his beer glass, Cal tried not to look too wolfish. "Okay. I want her."

JUNIPER COULDN'T REMEMBER when the bay had sparkled with such beauty and energy. Or perhaps it was just her seeing it that way. Standing out on the flagstone terrace of her tiny cottage on the mid-Maine coast, her third day there, she felt free. That surprised her. She was alone. Unemployed. Estranged from her uncle. Rather obsessed by a man common sense told her to forget about. In hiding, even. She should be desolate.

And yet, strangely, she wasn't. There were red roses growing along the rail fence in front of the terrace, and she could smell their light scent, mingling with the saltiness of the ocean. She had decided to spend the entire summer here, not just a week or two. For the first time in years she would truly have time to relax and contemplate whatever she felt like contemplating. It had been a long time since her life had been wholly her own. She would plant summer squash and tomatoes and marigolds. Maybe some broccoli, too. That would be nice. Fresh broccoli casserole and sliced tomatoes for supper in August.

No more impossible hours at the office. No more eating a late supper of some frozen gourmet dinner, then upstairs to her home office for more work. No more briefcases stuffed full of things to do over the weekend. No more fretting about whether Summerfield wouldn't show up—or whether he would. No more bucking the eccentricities of the Killibrew clan. "You're not like the rest of them," people had often told her. It was true. She wasn't. Wherever she went from here, people wouldn't know her or the Killibrews. She would be an unknown, blissfully anonymous.

Bo was barking at a snail out on the rocks. There was no sandy beach here, only a wide semicircle of huge rocks in front of her cottage, and the water was deep, the currents strong. The cats had installed themselves in sunny, screened windows overlooking the ocean.

Yes, Juniper thought, she would enjoy a peaceful summer here.

The cottage itself consisted of a small living room, kitchen, bathroom and bedroom. There was a big window in the living room that looked out across the terrace and the yard and the rocks to the bay, and a granite fireplace, and an old rocking chair she'd bought for eight dollars at a flea market and recaned, and ugly afghans made by a well-intentioned aunt on her mother's side, and an oak rolltop desk. A picture of Grandpa Killibrew hung above the fireplace. It was a famous one: he was riding a wild bronco or some such in New Mexico. That the horse had thrown him seconds after the picture had been snapped, landing him in traction for six months, made no difference. Here he was brash and victorious. That was how everyone remembered him.

Juniper had refused to hang the thing in her house, but here in Maine it was all right.

The light was beginning to fade; a chill was coming into the air. It was still spring in Maine, along the stretch of isolated coast north of Mt. Desert Island, where Grandpa Killibrew, in a fit of who knew what, had decided to buy land for his two sons. Summerfield still had the largely unused cottage next door. His brother had long ago abandoned his to Juniper, who used it whenever she could, in recent years all too infrequently.

She went inside and built a fire and made herself supper from her newly stocked refrigerator, and then she fed the cats and the dog and gathered them around her in front of the fire. In a little while she dozed off in the rocking chair, thinking of profit-and-loss columns, the winter catalog, the wallpaper that needed scraping and the possibilities of the South Pacific . . . and what life might be like if she ever decided to be partners with a rogue like Calvin Gilliam.

That brought her up short. A partnership was a compromise at best. At worst, just another ruse to get her securely under his thumb. She was in no mood to compromise and would never permit herself to be manipulated. Her heart pounding at her treacherous weakening, she made her way to bed. Her room was small and cozy, the bed a double, the headboard situated in front of the window so the sunrise would wake her. Up here, she had no digital clocks or shades or anything that would tell her when everyone else was getting up and going to work.

She was alone. She was free.

"SHE'S HAD THREE DAYS, Sum," Cal told his friend impatiently over the telephone that evening. "You asked me to give her some time to cool off, and I have. But as far as I can see, she's packed up her critters and taken off."

"Pulling a Grandpa Killibrew." Sum sounded worried. "That's not like her, Cal. Maybe I underestimated her anger."

Cal sighed. To his annoyance, he envisioned yet again the cool look Juniper had given him from behind the roses he'd sent her, a well-intentioned but ill-advised move on his part. He'd had moments like this before— all week, in fact. Moments when he couldn't seem to get her out of his mind, when he saw her so very vividly. It was quite ridiculous. "She's not coming back," he said.

"She *has* to. People at Traders are loyal to Juniper—the place will fall apart without her."

"I wouldn't go that far."

Sum was deadly serious. "She's not going to be easy to replace."

Sitting on the big bed at the inn, Cal realized he was getting tired of staying there, tired of feeling so ill at ease. What was wrong with him? Why the devil did he feel like an "incomparable rogue," when all he'd done was help out a friend? Why did he give a damn what saucer-eyed Juniper did with her life? He shook off the thought.

"I'm going after her," he said, hearing the ominous note in his voice.

So did Sum. "Cal? Are you— You wouldn't do anything drastic, would you?"

"Like tell her where you're sinking your profits?"

There was a pause on the other end of the line. "I know you better than that. Contrary to what Auntie Killibrew thinks, you're a man of your word."

Auntie Killibrew, the salty old woman of the straw hats and rogues. At least Cal could be grateful *she* hadn't been by to pester him again, although he suspected she was keeping firmly abreast of developments. "To answer your question," he said evenly, "I have no intention of doing anything drastic. In fact, if I had my way, you'd be the one to track down Juniper and persuade her—"

"Forget it. I'd be lucky to get out alive. Besides, you know I can't leave Portsmouth now."

"I know, dammit."

"Cal, why do I have a feeling you're not exactly unhappy I can't go after Juniper?"

"Because you have a fertile imagination," Cal snapped. "I just want to talk to her. Maybe she's had time to cool off and she'll listen. It's strictly business, Sum."

"Nothing's strictly business with you, Cal."

That was the problem with friends, Cal thought; they tended to know you pretty well. "Yes, well, it's too late to argue, isn't it? You've already told me where she is."

"And you've jotted it down in that steel-trap mind of yours."

"Absolutely."

"Well, there's one thing you don't know."

"She keeps a dragon in a cave on the beach?"

"No, although it wouldn't surprise me. I have a cottage there, too, Cal—right next door to hers."

Unable to suppress a grin, Cal stretched out his long legs. "Well, well, well."

THE NEXT MORNING Juniper rose with the sun. It was so quiet. She took a mug of coffee and walked down to the rocks in front of the cottage. The sunlight glistened on the water, and the buoys for the lobster pots, all marked with their fisherman's colors, bobbed in the rippling waves. The sky was soft with the pastels of sunrise. Juniper breathed in the clear air, filled with the smells of the ocean. It was low tide. Jumping from one giant granite boulder to another, she made it to the seaweed- and barnacle-covered rocks, usually under water at high tide, and looked at the tide pools that remained in the crevices.

She picked her way among the lower rocks, studying tide pools along the way, until she was below Summerfield's cottage. Just above her, a huge, flat boulder sat in the morning sun. She decided she'd finish her coffee there.

But as she climbed up onto the dry rocks, she was struck by something different about her uncle's red-shingle chalet. She wasn't sure what it was. She'd walked around out here yesterday and the day before, and nothing had seemed strange to her. Why did it now?

Then she saw it: all the shades were pulled down. Upstairs, downstairs. Not a single ray of the sunrise would penetrate the cottage.

It hadn't been like that yesterday.

So, she thought indignantly, Summerfield had decided to sneak off here with his ill-gotten millions!

Tossing the remains of her coffee in the grass, she slipped around back to make sure her uncle's car was parked there rather than one of his friend's. If he'd lent the place to someone else, she wouldn't want to make a fool of herself by barging in.

The car parked in the shade of an oak wasn't Summerfield's BMW. It was a gray Mercedes. A 450SL. Virginia license plate.

"I'll be damned," she muttered.

Refusing to stop and think, Juniper ran around to the front of the cottage and stomped up onto the porch. She set her mug down on the rail and, making a fist, pounded on the door.

Nothing happened. There were no curses from inside. No shades flipped up on angry looks. No shotgun poked out an opened window. No nothing. He was probably still asleep.

Good, she thought, and pounded some more.

Still she jumped back, startled, when the door was snatched open.

He stood there, staring at her, wearing nothing but a pair of shamefully close-fitting jeans. With a sharp intake of air she noticed the bronzed, hairy chest and the firm flesh around his belly button, and then the dark look in those pale-blue eyes. She should have thought of this, she reasoned now. She should have remembered how vivid and alive and very sexy this man was. A rogue, Auntie Killibrew had said. Juniper should have remembered.

But she recovered her poise quickly and glared back at him. "What are you doing here?" she demanded.

He appraised her frankly, making her aware, if not self-conscious, of her own less than scintillating dress. Hot-pink sweatpants and a red hooded sweatshirt. When one was alone on the rocks, one didn't care whether one clashed. However, when one was being surveyed by a sexy scoundrel just roused from slumber....

Good God, she thought, *I'm beginning to sound like Auntie.*

"I was sleeping," Cal Gilliam said mildly.

There was only a slight emphasis on *was*. Juniper immediately refused to think what he might be thinking—who could tell anymore?—and demanded, "Why here? Why not in Portsmouth or New York or Virginia—"

"No reason to sleep in any of those places."

She crossed her arms, annoyed with herself for noticing the purely sensual note in his casual drawl. "And you do have a reason for sleeping here?"

"Of course." He smiled. "I wanted to see how your memoirs are coming along."

"Liar."

"We always seem to be arguing through screens," he said, the smile reaching his eyes. "Now that I'm up, would you care to come in? We can have breakfast together. I brought brioche and eggs with me."

She thought of the thin-sliced whole wheat bread she had planned on eating for breakfast—not brioche, to be sure. But, she reasoned, she had never been one to walk purposely into a snake pit. That was for Grandpa Killibrew. Shaking her head, she said, "No, thank you."

He looked at her. "Then why are you pounding on my door at dawn?"

Her eyes narrowed. "*Your* door? I suppose now you're ready to snatch Summerfield's cottage out from under him?"

"You're a suspicious sort, aren't you?"

"Yes."

He laughed. "I do admire people who know themselves. But you're wrong. I have no intention of buying this place, however nice it is. Now either come in or go away—it's cold standing here."

Dressed as he was, she supposeed it would be. Her eyes involuntarily dropped to his chest, his waist, his lean hips, his thick thighs, his bare feet. No wonder she hadn't been able to get him off her mind; he was intensely memorable. When she returned her gaze to his face, he was grinning knowingly. Irritated, she said, "I'll just go away, then."

"Fine. Do."

"And you? What're you going to do?"

He lifted his shoulders. "Go back to bed."

Bed. No, she *wouldn't* envision him upstairs, lying naked under the slanted ceiling.... "Then what?"

"Have breakfast."

He was being obtuse—on purpose, she realized. He knew very well she wanted to know how long he planned to stay in Maine. "I mean, what are your long-range plans? How long do you intend to stay here?"

"I don't know. As long as necessary, I suppose."

"As necessary for what?"

"That all depends."

This just wasn't the time, she decided, to press him. Besides, she could easily guess what he was up to: he wanted her back at Killibrew Traders. He wasn't used to people turning their backs on him and walking out. He was relentless and didn't like to be thwarted. *Thwarted*, she thought. *Here I go again sounding like Auntie.* But where Cal Gilliam was concerned, it was difficult not to. As far as she could see, he was everything Auntie Killibrew had said he was.

"Well," she said, "I don't care what you do. Just plan on leaving me alone."

Not a single muscle of his hard body tensed as he nodded ever so slightly. If she aggravated him, he gave no indication. He was calm, casual, in control of himself.

"Pretend I'm not here," she added.

"As you wish."

"Don't bother me." She wanted to be dead sure he understood.

If she hadn't been looking for it, she might have missed the subtle gleam in his eyes. "Naturally I wouldn't want to disturb the flow of your creative energy."

His tone was sincere, but the rest of him wasn't. Juniper sighed. "Good," she said, grabbing her mug and marching off.

Back at her cottage, she let Bo out and urged him to prance next door and bite a hole in Cal Gilliam's well-worn jeans, but the ungrateful beast merely curled up on the warm rocks of the terrace and went to sleep. She fixed herself a breakfast of toast and orange juice and tried not to think about brioche and eggs and conversation with Gilliam and the night's growth of beard on the angular lines of his face and . . .

She just wouldn't think.

Well, he'd tracked her down. She wasn't so naive as to think the presence of Calvin Gilliam within spitting distance was anything but planned. But now what? Was he going to hog-tie her in the middle of the night and cart her back to Killibrew Traders? Or persuade her to return?

She went out onto the terrace and sat with Bo. She wouldn't want Calvin Gilliam to set his mind on persuading her to do anything. That just wouldn't do. It would be too distracting, not to mention unnerving. But there was nothing to be done about his being here. She couldn't very well run him off. She would just have to outlast him, that was all.

"That's right," she told Bo. "I'm more stubborn than he is. Damned if I'm going to leave. Hell, no. *He* can be the one to leave!"

THERE WAS NO BRIOCHE, and he had no eggs. That much had been a lie, but Cal had known Juniper wouldn't set foot inside the cottage with the shades all pulled and him in nothing but jeans. She was no fool, Juniper Killibrew. She knew there were sparks between them, just as he did. They'd been there the day of the tulip festival. They were there now. Maybe they'd go away of their own accord, but he didn't think so. The more he saw of her, the more he wanted her—if it was possible to want her more than before.

Wanting a spitfire like that wasn't like him, and he intended to remain very, very wary of unbidden sparks of sexual electricity.

He tried sleeping, but couldn't. Who was he kidding? If he didn't want the sparks to erupt into something more, then why was he here? Why didn't he just let Juniper Killibrew go off and write her memoirs and be done with her? He could handle any problems her departure from Killibrew Traders might cause. Despite her obvious beliefs to the contrary, he was no slouch in the executive department.

Then, as he stared out at the sparkling ocean, acceptance finally came. He wasn't here on this isolated, starkly beautiful stretch of coastline because of Killibrew Traders or his friendship with Summerfield or the warning he'd had from the old aunt.

He was here because of Juniper Killibrew. Period.

"Oh, *hell.*"

After putting on a shirt and a pair of sneakers, Cal drove into town for breakfast. He would have to be very careful. No doubt about that. He had a reasonable hold on Killibrew Traders but none whatsoever on its former vice president of marketing—and he wanted them both, the profitable catalog company and the elusive Juniper.

He'd always wondered if he wanted too damned much out of life. Or maybe that wasn't it at all. More likely he'd been hanging around Killibrews too long, and their weirdness was rubbing off on him. He was in the wilds of Maine, wasn't he, with a woman who claimed to be writing her memoirs?

IT WAS HOT by midafternoon. Juniper changed into a pair of shorts and a brightly colored bandeau which, at her insistence, had appeared in the summer catalog, a departure from the firm's reliance on traditional but rather dull skirt swimsuits. Even a chunky woman, she had reasoned, could successfully wear a bandeau with shorts or slacks or whatever. Bandeaus were sexy, she'd said; people liked to be sexy, especially in summer.

She told herself *she* was wearing a bandeau now because she wanted to be cool, not sexy. She felt an unexpected pang deep down; she missed Killibrew Traders.

Determined not to let her mood slide into depression, she sat out on the rocks with clipboard and pad in her lap and watched the tide roll in. Not for the first time that day, she glanced toward the neighboring cottage but, again, saw no sign of Cal Gilliam. The shades were up. The Mercedes was parked out back. But there was no Cal.

She had a vision of him up in the loft bedroom with a pair of binoculars trained on her and her bandeau. She was beginning to regret having put it on. His presence had an unsettling effect on her, making her think of herself in physical terms, not just mental. That would have been fine if he were any ordinary, sexy, attractive man. But he wasn't. He was Calvin Gilliam.

And she wasn't going to think about him right now.

At the top of a clean, blue-lined yellow page, she printed the block letters ACCOMPLISHMENTS. This was her first attempt at seriously revising her résumé. Of course, she had never intended to write her memoirs—she needed a job. The memoirs bit had just been to mislead Gilliam, a touch of the Killibrew in her, perhaps.

After a while she heard a screen door bang and peered across the rocks to the neighboring cottage. Gilliam walked out onto the porch and stretched, reaching his long arms straight up above him. He was wearing little navy-blue shorts and a white-mesh sleeveless shirt, and she could see the play of muscles in his legs, even from that distance. If he were plotting another chapter in his nefarious scheme to get her back to Traders, he didn't look it. He looked relaxed and perfectly at home at Summerfield's cottage. She watched him trot down onto the rocks. He had a fishing pole. Amazed, she clipped her pen to her pad as he cast his line out into the churning water. Just what did he think he was going to catch? A shark, she hoped. But he seemed intent on what he was doing, and she forced herself to resist the outrageous impulse to join him.

She went on listing her accomplishments. He fished.

And, occasionally, she glanced down toward the rocks. His back was to her, and he was a good fifty yards away, well down to her right. As far as she knew, he never once looked up in her direction. He must not have realized she was out there, and so she just stared whenever she pleased. He had such nice hips. And when there was a breeze, his hair blew every which way. It was disconcerting, having him so close by. If only—

No. She wouldn't get into any if only's. He was who he was, she was who she was, and what was done was done.

"Damn you, Summerfield," she muttered, "it's all your fault."

Gilliam didn't catch anything, and when he finally turned to head back up to his cottage, he grinned at her and waved, as if he'd known all along she'd been stealing looks. She pretended to be studying a point beyond him and didn't wave back.

The breeze carried his deep, full-bodied laugh all the way to her, and she growled in irritation.

Then he was behind her. She didn't know how he did it—she could have sworn he'd gone inside, and she never heard so much as a twig snap—but there he was now, casting his shadow over her as he jumped lightly onto her boulder. His legs were just as bronzed as his chest, and the assorted muscles in them were impressive. There was no ignoring his thighs, either. They were hard and thick with well-developed muscles, but lean, too, not the bulky thighs of a bodybuilder. Her face grew hot as she imagined them wrapped around her.

"Accomplishments?" He sat down right beside her unselfconsciously, their hips almost touching. He leaned over. "What's this for—your memoirs?"

"Have to begin somewhere." She flipped the page back so he couldn't see her list. She didn't want him to know she was job hunting. It would only fuel his fire, since he'd already offered her an ideal job: president and CEO of Killibrew Traders at twice her salary. What the devil was the matter with her? Why didn't she take it? She huffed and reminded herself of her principles.

"It won't work," she told him abruptly. "I'm not going back."

He looked out toward the bay and stretched out his legs, wiggling his toes, seemingly unconcerned about anything. He was barefoot, and she wondered just exactly what his scheme—she was positive he had one—to lure her back to the Killibrew fold would include. Seduction? She would have to be on her guard.

"You think that's why I'm here?" he asked.

"Of course. Why else?"

"Vacation."

"On an isolated stretch of coastline? With me conveniently as your neighbor? Not your style, Mr. Gilliam, and too coincidental."

"Maybe I want to write my memoirs."

"I doubt that."

"It is pretty isolated up here, isn't it?"

"Not as isolated as I'd like it to be."

That brought his eyes back to her; they narrowed as he studied her, but she didn't flinch.

She did feel oddly warm, though. "I make you nervous," he said flatly.

It was a statement of fact, but she said, "Not at all. You're just a distraction."

Up close, she saw that his grin emphasized all that was wrong with his face, its lack of symmetry, the day's growth of heavy beard, the prominent eyebrows, the lines at the corners of his eyes, the small deep scar on his forehead near his hairline. But the grin, rakish and brash, also brought out all that was right, the warmth, the intensity, the pale eyes. He burned with bridled passion, and for the first time it occurred to Juniper that this was no ploy. Cal Gilliam wanted her.

"Good," he said, very quietly.

She sighed and tore her gaze away, fighting to digest this new realization. He could only want her physically and even then for none of the right reasons. She was a challenge to him. An obstacle. Being a rogue, he would be aroused by that. All easy enough to analyze, she thought, but it solved none of the problems. He was here, she couldn't force him to leave and, to make matters worse, *he* aroused *her*. This was all much too complicated and dangerous, she decided, straightening. "Mr. Gilliam—"

"Cal, all right? No more Mister." His grin deepened. "Makes me nervous."

"Cal, then." But she used a Mr. Gilliam tone and hoped she exasperated him—and made her point. She was determined to keep her distance, and she wanted him to know it. "I came here for peace and quiet, and I would like you to respect that."

"I do respect it."

She didn't believe him. "Then perhaps we can get along if—"

"But," he added, rising to his feet, "I have no intention of paying any attention to it. Dinner tonight?"

She gritted her teeth. "No."

"I was going to grill salmon steaks."

"Good—do it."

He dusted his palms together. "I have enough for two."

"Then I hope you have a big appetite."

"You can't work all the time, Juniper."

Damn. She adored the way he drawled her name. It was downright delicious.

"Strike a deal," he said. "Have dinner with me to-night, and I'll leave you alone all day tomorrow."

Noting that he wasn't mentioning tomorrow night, she shook her head. "No deal."

He stared down at her. "Determined to steer clear of me, aren't you?"

She shrugged. "Not especially. I just want to do what I came here to do. I'm self-disciplined, you know."

"Mmm."

She could see he didn't believe her. But in addition to the smugness in his tone—all rogues were know-it-alls, Auntie Killibrew would say—there was something else, too. She couldn't quite place what. He sounded distracted . . . but that wasn't exactly it, either. The man confused her!

"Thank you for the dinner invitation," she said formally, wanting now to be rid of him. She had to collect her thoughts, establish a firm strategy for dealing with him.

He smiled. "There'll be others."

And off he went at a cocky pace. She supposed the deal was off altogether now. He *wouldn't* leave her alone all day tomorrow.

"That's it!" she said aloud.

She was like a company he wanted to take over, a company he wanted but whose board of directors didn't want him. This courting of her—it was like a bid for an unfriendly takeover. The company itself didn't drive Gilliam as much as the challenge of getting it, the fact that he wasn't wanted. *That* was what he found so invigorating. He throve on challenge.

And she had presented him with one. She had quit Killibrew Traders when he hadn't wanted her to quit. Now he would woo her back, come what may.

Then was wanting her a part of that? Had she presented him with more than a professional challenge? No, she must have misread his reaction to her, colored it with her own response to him.

Calvin Gilliam was unorthodox, it was true, and she didn't trust him, but even he wouldn't try to capitalize on the sexual tension between them and use it as a weapon to get her to return to her duties at Killibrew Traders.

But wasn't that what a true rogue would do?

She sighed. "He's here, isn't he?"

A point to consider. In the workaday world, Juniper knew, this sort of thing just didn't happen.

She went inside, typed a memo, tiptoed over to his cottage and shot it under his door. It said, "I suggest you avoid any taint of sexual harassment. I'll sue."

But she knew she was taking a chance that her note might only further galvanize Gilliam into action. Yes, he definitely liked a challenge. Right now, she was it.

6

THE NEXT DAY Juniper was out in the terrace combing Bo's tail when Cal—to her distress, she thought of him as Cal now, not just Gilliam—climbed up the rocks toward her. It was as if he'd materialized out of the sea, although she knew better. For one thing he was dry, dressed simply but devastatingly in thin white cotton pants and a pale-turquoise pullover. His old sneakers looked as if they'd been out tramping about the rocks of the Maine coast for years.

Juniper was ready with a quip about pirates and shipwrecks, but his serious look stopped her. He came onto the terrace and stood next to an old metal chair that had a little pile of golden dog snarls on the seat. He didn't seem to object. Running one finger along the rusted top of the chair, he said, "You're right, Juniper."

It wasn't the comment she'd expected. Loosening her firm grip on Bo's tail, she sat on the cool rocks of the terrace and tucked her legs into a tailor squat. Bo saw his chance to escape and slunk off. Juniper smiled up at Cal. "It's one of my more annoying habits," she said. "I'm often right."

Only his eyes moved. "And humble, too."

She shrugged. "I know my virtues as well as my vices."

"Name a vice."

"A quick temper." She spoke with a smile but meant what she said. In a way, it was an apology for last night. She had decided perhaps she didn't want to alienate Cal Gilliam, after all. She wasn't sure why; she had refused to let her thinking go that deep.

"Mmm." He shifted his weight from one leg to the other and dropped his hand from the chair down to his side. "Well, in this case you had every reason to get angry. I *have* been behaving like a cad."

She couldn't stop herself from grinning. "Cad?" You sound like Auntie Killibrew."

"Yes," he said dryly, "I suppose 'cad' would be on the list of names she has for me. But nonetheless, this time you do have a point. Of course, you can't bring charges of sexual harassment against me, since you're no longer employed by Killibrew Traders—and, in any case, I feel like the victim in this situation. You're the one who's put me on the spot by abandoning your post. Nevertheless, I'm willing to be reasonable."

She pulled dog hair out of the comb and added it to the pile on the chair while considering his comment. If she was going to be honest with herself, and she usually was, she had to admit she didn't think "reasonable" was in Calvin Gilliam's working vocabulary, at least not for his own conduct. She decided it might be wise to remain on her guard. "Thank you," she said politely. "I think."

He seemed satisfied with her response. "So we'll just be friendly neighbors."

There was always a catch. She noted the flash of victory in his eyes, the love of the chase, the challenge. To her surprise, her heartbeat quickened. Was she responding in kind? Was he a challenge to her? She was always trying to figure him out, wasn't she, to stay a step ahead of him. *No,* she thought, *don't be stupid. He's an irritant, if a sexy one. Once a cad, always a cad.* "Neighbors," she repeated cautiously.

"That's right." He was positively jaunty now. "I won't use any personal means to persuade you to return to Killibrew Traders."

Her brow furrowed. "Then you've accepted my resignation?"

"With regret."

"I see. And how long are we to be 'neighbors'?"

"Until— I don't know, actually." His eyes sought hers, and he smiled ever so slightly, which had the effect of making her palms sweat. He said mildly, "Until I tire of Maine."

"What about Killibrew Traders?"

"In good hands."

"But not yours."

"No. I've hired Arthur Green."

"The management consultant?"

"Then you know him?"

He wasn't surprised that she did, Juniper noted, just curious. "Only by reputation," she replied.

"He's very good."

"In his own way, I suppose."

"And he owes me."

She gave him a cool look. "I imagine many do." But she was surprised at her own reaction. She was anxious. Worried. Even upset. What would this Arthur Green do to her company?

It's not your company, she reminded herself. *It's Calvin Gilliam's company. And he can hire whom he pleases.*

"So, neighbor—" Cal was grinning, moving around the chair toward her "—How 'bout dinner tonight?"

A disturbing thought struck her. Cal wasn't going to leave Maine until she acquiesced...or at least appeared to give in. Stubborn as he was, he would have to see for himself that she really did intend to spend her summer here and never but never return to Killibrew Traders. Until then, he wouldn't accept her resignation. In that case she might be wise to play along, just a little. He might give up more easily—and more quickly.

And, of course, at dinner she might learn more about this Arthur Green and what he planned to do to the company. Her interest wasn't proprietary—she had no stake in Killibrew Traders—but simply professional. Or so she told herself.

"Okay." She climbed to her feet and even managed a smile. "Dinner tonight."

When Cal smiled back at her, there was no sign of victory or gloating, only pleasure. As if he truly wanted her company. As if by accepting, she'd made his day. He was good, she thought. Very good.

"Seven, then," he said, and leaped back down onto the rocks.

Maine was getting to him, she decided. Or to her.

IN HER KILLIBREW TRADERS exclusive pinpoint oxford cloth dress, bright fuchsia, with a white cotton sweater slung casually around her shoulders, Juniper took the easy route down the dirt driveway to her "neighbor's" cottage. Her hair was still slightly damp from her shower, and she'd dabbed on just a little Rive Gauche. She'd told herself she didn't want to smell like Bo. But she suspected it was more than that. All day she hadn't been able to get Cal out of her mind. And tonight she kept imagining what dinner would be like. What they would say. How she would feel afterward. It was disconcerting. She hadn't been able to get much done.

"Aren't you sexy tonight," Cal said with a grin, opening the front door wide. "Welcome."

Welcome to the snake pit, she thought, and wondered if she should thank him for the compliment.

Did that make any sense? She sighed. She just wasn't sure anymore.

She said hi and handed him two red roses that she'd picked from the bush growing along her terrace. His gaze locked with hers as he took the flowers from her—just for a second or two, but it was enough. She saw in his eyes something even more disturbing than gloating or the thrill of a challenge. He was touched by her gesture.

Hell, she thought, *no more roses*.

She couldn't afford to arouse feelings in Calvin Gilliam that he wasn't accustomed to having. And she realized, to her surprise, she was more comfortable dealing with the rogue in him. She didn't want to have to confront any sensitive individual that might be lurking beneath the cad. How Killibrew of her, she thought, amused.

Cal put the roses into a glass of water and placed them on the table, already set with Summerfield's mismatched, plastic dinnerware. Except for a small back bedroom and bath, the downstairs was open, only a counter separating kitchen and living room. It wasn't as cozy as Juniper's cottage and lacked her uncle's personal touch. He spent very little time there and often loaned the place to friends. Summerfield had legions of friends.

It was a cool, pleasant evening, and Cal had built a small fire in the stone fireplace. Juniper went over to it and pretended to warm her hands, but she was already strangely warm all over. Glancing at Cal as he stirred something on the stove, whistling away, she wondered if she should tell him that he, too, looked sexy tonight. His lean, hard body was clad in his usual sneakers, close-fitting jeans and a deep-plum cotton shirt, the sleeves rolled up to just below his elbows. His hair was dark and shining. He looked fit and energetic and . . . sexy.

She decided not to tell him so.

"What have you been doing all day?" he asked, setting his wooden spoon on the counter.

"Oh, this and that." Combing the cats. Dusting all three pets with flea powder. Reading a paperback novel. Considering various formats for her résumé. Putting tonight out of her mind. "Relaxing a bit."

He poured two glasses of red wine, walked over to the fireplace and handed her one. "How're the memoirs coming?"

"Slowly."

"Hmm. You probably need a break from them, so your thoughts can simmer a while."

She sipped her wine. "Tonight is a break."

"I mean an entire day."

"I see."

He was standing close enough that she could smell the freshness of him, and she felt her chest tighten and her breathing grow shallow, but only for a moment. She took a big drink of wine and moved away, just a step or two. What had ever possessed her to come tonight? She could be having stew with Bo and the cats. A nice, normal evening. This was . . . not normal.

"I was thinking of driving out to Schoodic Point tomorrow and having a picnic." His voice was low and silky. "Thought you might want to join me."

Not on your life. "Suppose we get through dinner first? I'm still mad at you, you know."

He grinned. "I'm a hard person to stay mad at."

"Want to make a bet?"

It was just a quick statement, not meant seriously, but he leaned toward her and said, "Sure. What are the terms?"

What had she gotten herself into? "I'm hungry," she said, deliberately not answering him. "Is dinner ready?"

To her relief, he said yes.

He had fixed a magnificent but simple meal of lobster bisque, salad and oatmeal rolls. Dessert was Hancock County lemon sherbet. They spoke of nonthreatening things: the weather, the lobstermen, the wild blueberry barrens, the icy Maine waters. But Juniper was enthralled.

"You know," she said, "I can't remember the last time I had an ordinary conversation with someone. Chatting with Bo and the cats just isn't the same. They don't talk back."

"One would hope."

She laughed. "I guess I'd better start worrying if they do, huh?"

"A sign of too many hours in the company of critters."

"I suppose. Well, Cal, it's been lovely. You can be nice when you put your mind to it."

"So can you."

She shrugged. "I guess we both have our nasty streaks."

But he was looking at her, studying her closely through narrowed cornflower eyes, and she had no idea at all what he was thinking. She could guess, of course—but she didn't want to. He said quietly, "Maybe I should walk you home now."

As abrupt as the suggestion was, there was nothing in his tone or his look to suggest he wanted her to leave . . . quite the contrary. They were both warm and full and feeling inclined toward each other, off their guard. If she stayed much longer, she knew she would end up there until morning. She wasn't ready for that.

"I can see myself back." She was surprised at how breathless she sounded.

"Of course you can." He rose. "But just the same, I could use a dose of cold air right now."

"Sleepy?"

"Hardly."

It was amazing, she thought, how damned *stupid* she could be at times! She got up quickly and decided not to offer to help with the dishes.

Outside there was a stiff, cold, damp wind blowing off the ocean. Juniper slipped on her sweater. Cal had pulled on a hooded sweatshirt. Damn, she thought, he was one striking man. It would be so easy to get involved with him—but pointless. Brief, heated affairs weren't her style, and she knew there could be nothing more between them. Except physically, he wasn't her type, and she wasn't his. He owned Killibrew Traders; she didn't. He was willing to use Summerfield to get what he wanted; Juniper had only ever wanted to help her uncle.

Pointless, she repeated to herself. And she wasn't one to do anything that had no point.

They took the long route, along the rocks, finding their way in the starlight.

"It's beautiful out here," Cal said softly.

"Yes."

He stumbled as he jumped across a deep, narrow crevice to a boulder, and her hand shot out automatically, grabbing his upper arm to steady him. His hand quickly covered hers. The hard, tensed muscle under her palm slowly relaxed, and she jumped lightly to the spot next to him.

She could see his smile in the night. "Thanks," he said.

"Wouldn't want to have to scrape you off the rocks."

"A romantic thought." He was being mildly sarcastic.

Juniper couldn't seem to get enough air, and what she got only added to her uneasiness. "I know, I'm trying to spoil the mood."

"Why?"

That was Cal, she realized, always pushing, probing, demanding answers to questions better left unasked, never mind answered. And it was Juniper's nature to answer a question put to her, not to shy away. She had never been good at acting coy. She shrugged. "Because otherwise we might kiss or something," she said casually, "and I don't think either of us wants that."

He laughed softly—a low, sandpapery sound she wanted to go on forever. "I think 'or something' would be virtually impossible out here on the rocks, don't you?"

"I suppose it would." She smiled at the thought, and before she could think not to, whispered, "But a kiss wouldn't."

"No." His hand dropped from hers. "A kiss wouldn't."

His arm, solid and warm, slid around her waist, and she drew closer, because she wanted to, not because she couldn't stop herself. She was clearheaded about that. Although she didn't trust Calvin Gilliam with Killibrew Traders or her uncle, she trusted him with herself. She smiled, thinking of it. When he wasn't being the corporate raider and she wasn't being the indignant vice president, they were fine together. Neighbors, she thought, as they brought their mouths together.

His lips were moist and soft and warm, and she felt her heartbeat quickening and an ache starting deep inside her and spreading. She wanted this man. With a start she realized she had wanted him from the moment she'd spotted him, alone and inappropriate, at the tulip festival.

Their bodies were barely touching. She wanted to press herself to him, feel every inch of him, every muscle, every bit of bronzed skin. But she held back, touching just his upper arm. Even so, she could sense the heat coursing through him. He wanted her, too. This wasn't a lie.

Then it was over. In a choked whisper he said, "Good night," and was gone into the darkness. And she stood there, immobile, in a shaft of starlight. A gust of wind blew the cold right through her. She headed the rest of the way up to her cottage, then made herself a cup of soothing chamomile tea and sat in front of the big window in the living room for a long time, looking at the stars twinkling over the Atlantic.

CAL WAS ON THE LINE to Summerfield in Portsmouth. "How's it going?" Cal asked. "Any closer to being able to come clean with Juniper?"

"Getting there." Summerfield sounded cheerful. "I think this thing's going to work, Cal. How're you?"

"Surviving." He remembered last night, and the heat surged through him. He felt fatigue biting at him. Had he slept at all? Very little. Juniper had haunted him, whether he was awake or half-asleep. "Juniper thinks I've used you, you know, that you're the victim in this."

"She doesn't give me credit for having any plans and ideas of my own—never has. It's this fixation she has, I suppose, that she's so different from the rest of us. Look, Cal, I know I'm not making things any easier on you, but give me a little more time. Okay?"

"I'll do what I can."

"And Cal?"

"Yeah."

"Don't underestimate Juniper."

HE ARRIVED on her terrace promptly at eleven-fifteen the following morning, picnic basket in hand, and tapped on the window at her. She quickly shoved the want ads of the Boston *Sunday Globe* under her work table. Checking want ads, especially at her level, was not much of a way to find a job, but she was curious. There were jobs out there, to be sure. With her experience in the exploding catalog retail market, she could go lots of different places. Join the competition. Help them bring down Killibrew Traders.

What a traitor she was!

With a flip of the wrist she motioned for Cal to go away.

To her surprise he did—but only for a moment. He reappeared at her screen door. "Morning," he drawled. "May I come in?"

"No—I'm not dressed."

"Liar. I just saw you through the window. You're wearing a lavender shirt and little silver earrings and—"

She didn't want him to go on. "Okay, okay, but just for a minute."

She threw the sports section on top of the want ads just as he came through the door. The picnic basket swinging from one hand was an old one. "I remember when Summerfield and Auntie and I used to go on picnics together. Uncle would make sandwiches, I'd do dessert, and Auntie would do whatever struck her fancy—often nothing. We'd find a deserted, rocky shore, and she'd sometimes sit and read us Shakespeare."

"Odd," Cal said.

"That's Auntie."

He smiled. "It's a Killibrew."

"Not me. What have you got in there?"

"Nothing fancy: cold, broiled lime-tarragon chicken, potato salad, rolls . . ."

"You've been busy."

"Cooking helps pass the time. I made a fresh strawberry pie, too."

"A man of surprising talents."

He shrugged, moving closer to her. "There's no TV over there, no radio, only a few books—and no you, of course. What's a man to do to keep himself occupied?"

She snatched a pencil off her table to keep herself occupied. Otherwise she'd probably sit and wring her hands. "Bake pies, I suppose," she said.

"Tempted?"

"I'm human."

He leaned over her shoulder and peered down at the pad and clipboard on her work table. She'd drawn a few unintelligible scribbles on the pad, nothing that gave her away. "Still on chapter one? You need to rest your brain, Juniper."

He placed a hand on her shoulder. There was nothing remotely intimate about the gesture—he might have been a relative—but it still sent a tingle down her spine. "I promise," he said, mockingly grave, "I won't mention memoirs or Killibrew Traders. We'll just eat lunch and watch the waves. What do you say?"

She arched a look up at him. "What happens if I say no?"

"We eat out on the terrace."

"I thought so."

There was a greater likelihood of encountering people at Schoodic Point than there was on her terrace. That meant there was a greater likelihood that the picnic wouldn't digress into anything she might regret. Of course, she could banish him to his cottage. But that wouldn't be very neighborly.

"You'll drive? I'm low on gas."

He grinned. "Cheap Yankee."

They were fifteen minutes north of Schoodic Point, a part of Maine's Acadia National Park and a popular summer retreat. Schoodic was a mass of giant granite boulders, typical of the Maine coastline, but here the rocks got the full brunt of the Atlantic. There were none of the state's thirty-five hundred islands to impede the progress of the surf and, under the right conditions, the waves could be spectacular. They'd been known to toss rocks the size of grapefruit up into the woods.

That morning the tide was coming in at a pleasant, steady roll, and there wasn't another human being in sight, just them and the gulls and the ocean. They walked out on the rocks, close to the strand line, and watched in silence as wave after wave after wave crashed against the solid rock. To the southwest, the pink granite peaks of the more well-known Mt. Desert Island, which formed the bulk of Acadia, seemed to sparkle in the bright sun.

"Beautiful," Cal said.

"Yes."

Moving back a ways on the rock, they opened up the picnic basket, but inside there wasn't any lime-tarragon chicken, potato salad or rolls. Or, as far as Juniper could see, any strawberry pie. There were sandwiches wrapped in waxed paper and a bag of potato chips.

She glared at Cal. "That looks like peanut butter and jelly."

"It is."

"You lied."

"Indeed."

"You got me out here on false pretenses."

His eyebrows quirked. "You only came for the food?"

"Peanut butter and jelly is *not* lime-tarragon chicken."

"Haven't you heard of the power of positive thinking?"

She ignored him. "And where's my strawberry pie?"

"Oh, that." He whipped out the sandwiches and chips and lifted out the basket's false bottom. Underneath was, in fact, a strawberry pie. "There."

"You still lied."

"Persuaded."

"Lied."

"I'd have to have slaved for hours to make chicken and potato salad and rolls—"

"What kind of peanut butter is it?"

Now he glared at her. "What the devil do you mean, what kind of peanut butter? Peanut butter's peanut butter."

"No, it isn't. I don't like shortening and sugar and all that goop in my peanut butter."

"Good Lord." He frowned at her, the picnic basket and all the world between them. "What kind *do* you like?"

"All natural. Just peanuts in it. Crunchy."

He handed her the sandwich. "Then that's what's on this."

"I don't believe you."

He grinned. "The power of positive thinking, remember?"

She opened up the sandwich and bit into it. "Ycch."

"So it's not crunchy."

"It's not natural, either."

"Go on. You can't tell the difference."

She took another bite, contemplated the taste and, against her better judgment, swallowed again. "It's generic," she said. "Not even a brand name."

Cal stretched out his long legs and laughed.

"It is, isn't it?" she persisted.

"Well . . . I suppose. It's just what was hanging around."

"*Summerfield's* peanut butter?"

"I imagine so."

"It could be *years* old!"

"So? The stuff stays good forever."

"Lord!"

"What about the jelly?"

"It's Auntie's currant, isn't it?"

He laughed. "You do have discerning tastes, don't you?"

"In everything," she said, not really serious.

But he turned toward her, his eyes lost in the shadows cast by the bright sunlight. "In men, too?"

"In men in particular."

"You expect them to be as perfect as your peanut butter?"

She shook her head, determined to maintain an air of lightheartedness. "Just all natural, without a lot of extra fat and no sugars and syrups whatsoever."

At that Cal opened up his peanut butter sandwich, sighed, and ate. He winced. "It is pretty awful, isn't it?"

This time she laughed. "But edible."

"Barely. Shall we forego the sandwiches and dig into the pie?"

"Sounds good to me."

And they did, consuming nearly half the thing. Juniper told him he was a terrific cook, something she admired in people. "What about you?" he asked.

"Oh, I can do it when I put my mind to—I just don't very often."

"Too busy?"

"Usually. And it's more fun to cook for someone besides just yourself."

"I know what you mean." He leaned back on his elbows and watched a monstrous wave roll in, crash against the rocks and roll out again. "Did you do much cooking when you were a teenager, or did you have to learn on your own?"

"Oh, no. I was always brewing something. You?"

"I learned on my own. I come from one of those families where children only cooked at camp."

"How very proper. Did your mother do the cooking?"

"Heavens, no. We had a housekeeper."

"Ah."

"And my father cooked fish he'd caught, but that was about it."

"Do you have brothers and sisters?"

"A younger brother, Charles, and an older sister, Marilyn."

"What do they do?"

"They're bankers."

"Both of them?"

"I come from a long line of bankers."

"And you? Where do you fit in?"

He gathered up the papers and forks and plates and shoved them back into the basket, shutting it with more force than was necessary. "I don't."

There was nothing more to be said. Torn between wanting to know more, wanting to tell him about how she didn't fit in with her family, either, and not wanting to get any closer to him than she was, Juniper simply commented on the color of the ocean. Another couple was walking down onto the rocks. Another couple? No, *a* couple. She and Cal were just two hard-headed individuals. They weren't partners.

She jumped to her feet and beat him to the car. To her relief, he hardly spoke during the entire trip back to their cottages.

That evening, she stayed up late and did up a draft of her résumé. It was just a first step. She knew she couldn't get a job sitting up in Maine and picnicking with Calvin Gilliam, but she had to start somewhere— and soon.

Reluctantly she went upstairs to bed, feeling more alone than she'd felt in months. She snuggled up with the cats and listened to Bo breathing softly under the bed, and her mind wandered, picturing what it would be like to have Cal with her.

"That's why you've got to make a new future for yourself," she told herself reasonably. "He's getting under your skin."

Summer wasn't going to last forever. Sooner or later she and Cal would have to go their separate ways. That had been ordained from the beginning. Even if isolation could bring them together, there was nothing at all that could *keep* them together.

Nothing, she thought, and fell asleep.

7

CAL WAS AWAKE for the sunrise. He'd forgotten to pull the shades, and the sun, pale and golden, hit him in the face at dawn. But it was beautiful. He pulled on some clothes and headed down to the rocks, just to see the light dancing on the water. It was a romantic place, Maine. And he thought again of Juniper. Unbidden, his gaze turned to the left.

And there she was, out on a flat, sunlit boulder with her clipboard.

"Morning!" he yelled across the rocks.

She jumped slightly, startled, and then frowned in his direction. He laughed. What a scowl she had! Even from some thirty yards away, he could see how her face scrunched up, and he could almost hear her irritated sigh. "Prickly and poisonous," Sum had said. Well, Cal couldn't say he hadn't been warned.

He leaped across the rocks—he was starting to feel like a bloody mountain goat—and came up beside her. She flipped over her clipboard so he couldn't see what she was writing. Damn. He'd like to know what she was putting in her so-called memoirs: "How Killibrew Traders came into the hands of a pirate." And she didn't know the half of it, not that he was at liberty to tell her. In a way he wished she liked him, but he also had to admit, on a certain level, their animosity was exciting. Maybe old Ms Killibrew was right, and he was a rogue.

"I'm busy," Juniper said.

"Cranky, too."

She glared up at him, the wind in her hair, the sun in her glorious gray eyes. *Hell.* What was the matter with him this morning? *The same thing that was the matter with you yesterday, Gilliam, and the day before and every damned day since you set eyes on this enigmatic woman.* He couldn't get his mind off her. That was all. It was a fact. Simple. Inescapable.

"What do you want?" she asked.

He frowned down at her. "Are you trying to intimidate me?"

"No, I'm trying to work. Now what is it?"

"Can rogues be female?"

She almost laughed—he was sure of it—but she maintained her impressive self-control, a quality he admired in anyone, man or woman. But he wanted to concentrate on her faults, not her virtues. Her near laugh became a pleasant smile. "State your business, Gilliam," she said cheerfully.

He ran his toe along the very edge of the boulder. "Maybe I just came over to say hi."

"With you, nothing's ever that simple."

How true. He sat down beside her, their thighs not quite touching as he dangled his legs over the edge of the chunk of granite. Ever since the abrupt end of their picnic yesterday, he'd imagined those strong, lean legs of hers wrapped around his, and that presented another simple and inescapable fact: he wanted to make love to her. Desperately. *Now.* But that would only lead to personal pain for them both, and he wanted to avoid that. He, too, had a certain enviable measure of self-restraint.

"Well, as a matter of fact," he said, "I did wander over here for a reason. I'm leaving today."

Her eyes shot up at him, and for an instant he thought he saw something approaching disappointment in them, even panic, but then it was gone, and they were cool and politely curious. "Oh?"

"I'm driving down to Portsmouth. Then tomorrow morning I'll cruise down to New York for a couple of days. I've some business to attend to."

"I see."

"I thought you might want to know."

She shrugged. "I suppose."

"Do you want to know when I'll be back?"

"Not particularly."

"Maybe I'm not coming back."

Another shrug. "No skin off my nose."

"Juniper, you can be damned aggravating."

She looked at him. "What do you want me to say? 'Oh, Cal, don't go, I'll miss you so'? Really. That's not me."

A good point. "Well," he said irritably, "will you?"

"Will I what?"

"Don't be obtuse, woman. Will you miss me?"

Her smile was slight, sly and absolutely delicious. "Let's just say I'll notice your absence."

He patted her thigh—a mistake. He'd meant it only as a friendly gesture, even a taunt, but the feel of her warm, firm skin under his palm brought on all too familiar stirrings of passion. He snatched his hand away. "I will be back, you know," he said.

She brushed one finger along the top of his hand and let her smile broaden. "I know."

He would have kissed her, but she jumped up with her clipboard, and he decided there was nothing to do but just get moving. Portsmouth, New York—and then back here. Maybe. Seeing her now, aching for her, he wasn't sure it was such a good idea.

Then she surprised him. "Breakfast?"

He grinned. "What do you have?"

"Fat and cholesterol."

"Eggs and bacon?"

"You got it."

"How can I resist?"

And as he followed her up to her cottage, he thought; *How can I?*

They ate on the terrace, Juniper in her red sweatshirt and the black sweatpants that hugged her thighs. Looking at her, Cal knew he'd been with women more beautiful, but none more alive, more vibrant, more interesting, or more annoying. Being around her did things to him. He wanted to make love with her. He wanted to talk politics and life and business and ideas with her. He wanted to sit for hours with her, saying nothing.

Dangerous. It was good that he was leaving—better, perhaps, that he didn't come back.

"You seem preoccupied," she said quietly.

He smiled at her. They were sitting on the old metal chairs, their plates on their laps because there was no table. Juniper had pushed her chair so she was facing him at an angle. "Not used to getting up at this hour," Cal said, knowing it was a lame excuse. He wanted to lean over and just graze her mouth with his. See what would happen then. What she'd do. What she'd feel like. *Good God, man, stop!* He said quickly, "I should be going."

"Give my best to everyone at Traders."

Not, he observed, "Won't you stay for another cup of coffee?"

He rose. "Of course."

"Just leave your plate on the chair. I'll get it."

"Thanks."

She remained seated. "Have a good trip."

"You won't consider—"

Her eyes flashed. "Joining you? No."

"You're going to sit up here writing memoirs no one gives a damn about when you have a mind and experience—"

"Auntie cares about my memoirs."

"Auntie!" He turned on her. She blinked up at him and sipped her coffee. "Juniper, haven't you carried this thing far enough? You have every right to be furious with your uncle, but why make Killibrew Traders suffer? Why make yourself suffer?"

"Do I look as though I'm suffering?" To prove her point, she stretched out her legs and yawned, breathing in the fresh morning air. "In any case, what you mean is why make *you* suffer."

"Have it your way." Teeth clenched, he stalked off the terrace and started around the cottage toward the dirt road. He was leaving, dammit. Never coming back. Blasted woman. Who the devil was she to talk about rogues and cads? Let the Killibrews rot in their own stupid pride and family squabbles. *He* was finished with them.

Then he stopped and bit off a sigh. "The hell with it."

He turned sharply and bounded back to the terrace, where Juniper was still sitting stretched out and relaxed, coffee mug in her lap, eyes on the bay. Calm. Unperturbed. That irritated him more than anything.

"Juniper."

She glanced up.

Stifling another sigh, he walked over to her, bent down and planted a kiss, hard, on her mouth. There wasn't even a flicker of surprise in her gray eyes, more amusement than anything. "You're a difficult woman to figure out, you know that?"

"I know."

"Dammit, Juniper, I *will* be back."

Then he stalked off.

But as he rounded the cottage, her voice carried to him. "Don't come crying back to me if Killibrew Traders has gone to pot while I've been gone."

"In a week?" he yelled back. "Even you're not that good!"

He hoped. He'd sunk enough money and honor into this deal; all he needed now was to have it turn sour—especially because of her. Cursing Summerfield Killibrew and whatever made a Killibrew tick, Cal packed his things, climbed into his Mercedes and fled.

But he'd be back, if for no other reason than to see if the sexual tension between him and the former vice president of Killibrew Traders would have dissipated after a few days apart. He didn't think it would. No, he knew it wouldn't. But from Juniper's point of view? There was only one thing for certain: she had recognized the sparks between them for what they were.

"You're a fool, Gilliam," he said to himself. "That's the best reason of all for staying away."

FOR THE NEXT DAY and a half, Juniper was desolate. She moped. She took long walks. She sat on the rocks in front of Summerfield's cottage—Cal's cottage. She waited for someone to come out and join her, but no one did. All the shades were drawn. She was alone.

"Lord," she said aloud to no one, "what's wrong with me?" Exhaustion, she told herself. Post-resignation depression. Not enough work. She had lots of excuses, but together they amounted to a pack of lies.

What was wrong with her was Calvin Gilliam.

She thought of his wild hair lifting in the wind, his laugh, the way he walked, packed with energy and sexuality. She thought of their meals together and of how much she enjoyed being around him, arguing, taunting, laughing, talking. And she thought of what a pain she'd been. She regretted that now. Yet he seemed more intrigued by her faults than put off by them. It was the challenge she presented, of course, nothing more.

"You need a job," she said, and started up toward her cottage. She wasn't going to get one sitting in Maine and having picnics . . . and moping.

Auntie was right; it was the fate of Killibrew women to fall for rogues. "It's in your genes," she'd said. Juniper added silently, *Like a disease.*

CAL HAD HIS TROUBLES in Portsmouth, too, he discovered. Over a long, frank business lunch with Arthur Green, he listened to his interim president itemize the problems at Killibrew Traders. Most of them were hunches. "I don't have anything concrete," Arthur admitted. "Nothing's appeared on paper yet, but something's not going right around there."

It wasn't what Cal wanted to hear. "Just keep on going as you have, Artie. From what I hear, you and Juniper Killibrew have similar styles. Things should iron out."

"I don't know, Cal."

"You've always been a pessimist. Just hang in there, okay?"

Later Cal had dinner with Summerfield, who was in such high spirits that Cal didn't have the heart to tell him about Artie's negative hunches. He just kept quiet and listened. The sale had been good for Summerfield. Now if only Juniper could see that, accept it and move on to the future.

Auntie Killibrew was waiting for Cal in the formal parlor of the inn where he was staying. It was an old parlor, done entirely in Queen Anne, and the elderly woman looked as if she belonged there. She rose to greet Cal. "I only have a minute," she said. "I'll be leaving for my summer cottage on Mt. Desert Island tomorrow morning, and I wanted to be sure to speak with you first."

"How did you know I was in town?" Cal asked, pouring himself a glass of sherry. Auntie had already served herself a liberal glassful.

"Summerfield told me." The old woman narrowed her fierce eyes at him. "You look tired, Mr. Gilliam. I've been thinking perhaps I've misjudged you."

He smiled grimly. "I'm not such a rogue, after all?"

"Oh, I'm sure you are—but in the good sense."

Cal had no idea what she meant.

She sipped her own glass of sherry. "Mr. Gilliam, I think Killibrew Traders is on the verge of experiencing serious difficulties. The company needs Juniper, and

Juniper needs the company. It's a symbiotic relationship, you understand. It has been for years."

"Why are you telling me this? I didn't fire her, you know."

"I know." She rose, looking tall and regal and very concerned. "She's stubborn, and her pride has been wounded most grievously. However, I believe the situation can be corrected."

Cal just stared at her. "Any suggestions?"

"Why, get her back, of course." She walked to the doorway, then turned, fastening those steel-gray eyes on him. "If anyone can, it's you."

JUNIPER OCCUPIED HERSELF these days by taking long walks, doing lots of reading, eating too much and— miracles of miracles—compiling her résumé. And thinking of Cal. She tried not to—what was the point of it? Better to mail out résumés, which she did, on a bleak, foggy morning that promised to evolve into a bleak, foggy afternoon.

ON HER WAY to the mailboxes with her résumés, she noted the empty parking space next to Summerfield's cottage. So Cal wasn't coming back. Well, it was just as well. She placed her neatly stacked bundle of buff-colored envelopes in the mailbox, shut it and put up the flag. They'd be collected by midafternoon. She stood there a moment, realizing her throat was tight. *Damn*, she thought, *this is no time to get choked up.* But she couldn't help it. She *was* unemployed. She *had* quit her job. The company was sold, and she was out of work.

It was over.

The last of the Killibrews of Killibrew Traders was gone, and it wasn't fair. She was different from the others. She hadn't thumbed her nose at family tradition. She had worked so hard, believed so much. And for what? To be booted out.

You quit, remember? Of course. She'd had to. If she had stayed, she'd have ended up working with Calvin Gilliam. *Well, so? He'd fit right in with the Killibrew clan, wouldn't he? And you're used to working with Killibrews.* True, but Cal wasn't a Killibrew. There was no common blood to draw them together . . . or keep them apart.

With a shudder she trudged back to her cottage, where she built a cozy fire and, gathering her animals around her, sat. She was depressed. It had never been like this before. Never. She was Juniper Killibrew. She always knew where she was going and how she was getting there.

A new job. Direction. Work. That was what she needed. Tomorrow, she decided, she'd start playing her contacts. Enough of stewing in Maine and drawing up résumés and writing mythical memoirs. Within twenty-four hours the word would be out: Juniper Killibrew was available immediately . . . for damn near anything.

SHE HAD BECOME ATTUNED to every sound on this narrow piece of land, and the putter of an engine outside, right after lunch, wasn't that of a lobster boat or a lawn mower or a plane overhead. If she were guessing, and she supposed she was, she would say it was a car engine. Specifically, a Mercedes. Even more specifically, a Mercedes 450SL, pearl gray, Virginia license plate.

Laying the book she was reading on the mantel, Juniper got up. "So," she said, "the rogue returns." To her surprise, she laughed.

She peered out her kitchen window. The Mercedes looked stately and untouched by the gloom of the early afternoon, and so very Cal Gilliam in style. She saw him climbing out of the car. His hair was tousled and so dark, and he wore a navy-blue rugby shirt. Juniper acknowledged the lurch of her heart at seeing him again. She didn't accept it, didn't like it by any means, but merely acknowledged it as one of those dismal little facts one had to consider before arriving at a conclusion. She was good at that. The ability to look at all evidence with a cool eye was one of the things that made her a top-notch executive.

He kicked the door shut with the ball of his foot, and she noticed he was carrying something. A stack of papers, it looked like. No, envelopes. Buff-colored envelopes. About a hundred of them, neatly bundled up and held together by a heavy-duty rubber band.

"You bastard!"

She sprang out the back door, arms waving, face red, legs pumping hard down the dirt driveway. She knew she must look like a maniac, but she had no intention of reining in her temper. To hell with it. She was *furious*.

To his credit, Cal didn't try stuffing the envelopes under his shirt. He didn't even manage to look sheepish—didn't even try. He merely stood there with a sly smile on his striking face and acknowledged that he'd been caught. "Red-handed, as it were." His smile broadened. "Afternoon, Juniper"

She glared at him. "You stole my mail."

He eyed the bundle cradled in one arm and shrugged. "So I did."

"How dare you!"

"Isn't that a bit old-fashioned? How dare I. I dare, m'dear. Auntie Killibrew would like that, don't you think? M'dear? Nice ring to it. Something a rogue would say." A letter slipped out and fluttered to the ground. Neither moved to pick it up. Cal's pale-cornflower eyes were fixed on Juniper; he seemed to be enjoying himself. "I dare because—" he slowly grinned "—it's in my nature."

"Bastard that you are."

"Is that a degree or two worse than a rogue and a cad?"

She refused to answer him.

He shifted his weight, bending one knee slightly, a move that might have signaled unease but, on him, didn't. He was unperturbed and unrepentant. If anything, he seemed amused—even victorious. But what victory could he possibly have won?

"I could have you arrested," she said, trying now to sound sophisticated and indignant. "Stealing mail is a federal offense, you know."

He laughed. "I'd like to see you prove it. Even more, I'd like to see you explain our relationship to the authorities."

She kicked a stone and watched it skid by him. "I'm a normal, decent, law-abiding woman, and you're a blood-sucking mosquito. A disease-ridden tick. A parasite, a pest, a—"

"I prefer rogue and cad myself, even bastard."

"Damn you!"

"You're losing control, Juniper."

"You haven't seen anything yet! As far as I'm concerned—" she stopped suddenly and stared. "—you're grinning."

"Mmm."

"Grinning!"

"Can't help myself, m'dear." He swooped down and snatched up the stray envelope, straightened the bundle and thrust them against her chest. "Memoirs, my hind end. You, Juniper Killibrew, are job hunting."

And he strutted off, chuckling to himself.

JUNIPER ATE LEFTOVERS for supper that evening, all the while deciding she would never speak to Calvin Gilliam again. She briefly considered packing up her Volvo and continuing her job hunting in earnest from her house in Portsmouth, but she rejected the idea. She wasn't going to run. He would *not* drive her out. Besides, she had a feeling Gilliam would only track her down again. He was a tenacious rat.

She smiled to herself. Had she actually called him a tick? The vice president of marketing for a major catalog clothing firm, reduced to verbal sparring with a man who didn't deserve such energy. Well, at least she'd driven into town and mailed the letters herself. She could have tossed them into the sea, rolled up her sleeves, swallowed her pride and headed back to Killibrew Traders. Let the rogue/cad/bastard/tick/flea/rat win. No way.

Indeed. It was a victory, small but nonetheless a victory, that she'd mailed the things. Now she was focusing her attention on another small, private battle: persuading herself not to tramp across the rocks and ask the new owner of Killibrew Traders how his company was doing without her. She wasn't sure she wanted to know. Which would be worse? That Killibrew Traders was hurting because she'd left . . . or that it wasn't?

Either way, it didn't matter. She wouldn't be partners with Calvin Gilliam, not at any level.

There was a knock at her door, just one. She got up from her seat by the fire, saw it was Cal and told him to come in. He did, still in his jeans and rugby shirt but without the gleam of victory in his eyes.

"What do you want?" she asked, not sourly.

"I'd like to apologize."

He closed the door behind him. In the small living room he seemed even taller, his hair slightly damp from the ubiquitous mist. "I shouldn't have done what I did. It was inexcusable."

He was the Virginia gentleman now, all honest and sincere, and utterly irresistible. Juniper didn't know what to do with him. Relent? Demand an explanation? Invite him in for tea? No, she thought, looking at him, feeling her heart begin to pound. She would get rid of him—fast.

"It's okay," she said. "Apology accepted."

It was a dismissal, which he took with a surprised lifting of his eyebrows. "You're not going to ask me to explain?"

"No."

"You're nervous."

"Me? Don't be silly. Why you stooped to stealing my mail out of the mailbox seems fairly obvious to me, and in keeping with your reasons for being up here. You want me back at my post at Killibrew Traders. Okay, fine. You acted like an ass, I got mad, and now you've apologized. I accept your apology. So you can go."

He walked over and stood beside her in front of the fire, holding out his hands to the warmth. They were large hands, she noted, not heavily callused, but not soft, either, and the fingers were long and broad. She imagined them on her breasts.

"Something wrong, Juniper?"

"Just cold, I guess."

"You stiffened up."

"I know, dammit!"

He smiled over at her. "It's getting to you, too, isn't it?"

"What?"

"Being together."

"I'd hardly call what we are 'together.'"

"I know." He looked back at the crackling fire. "Maybe that's the problem."

"So why *did* you steal my mail?"

"I thought you had that all figured out."

"I'd like to hear it from you."

"You're changing the subject."

"Getting back to the subject." She stuck her hands into her pockets and sat back down. "Well?"

He didn't answer right away, and Juniper took the opportunity to admit to herself that she had changed the subject. With him she was more comfortable being angry. All this other stuff, passion and honesty and sensitivity, made her very *un*comfortable. She was doing things like noticing his hands, the way the mist glistened on his hair and the heart-stopping proportions of broad shoulders and lean hips. Lord, but she couldn't figure out this man—nor why she reacted to him as strongly as she did. Were they two of a kind? No. Impossible.

"I knew I had you," he said, still standing, hands warming. "I saw the flag up on the mailbox and just sensed you were up to something. It's that way between us, you know. I can feel things about you. It's never been like this with anyone else, not for me. But in any case, I looked in the mailbox, saw your bundle of résumés—"

"How did you know they were résumés?"

"They had that look about them—all one hundred or so of them."

He went on matter-of-factly, "And so I knew I had you. There are no memoirs—never were. You haven't bowed out of anything, Juniper Killibrew. You're job hunting. Knowing that, I wanted more than ever to be here to lure you back to Killibrew Traders, and to rub your nose in it a bit, too, I suppose. But your going back is what's best for the company and, I believe, what's best for you."

Juniper was ready with an acid remark but held back. Calvin Gilliam was worried about what was best for Killibrew Traders, which surprised her. And it pleased her. And, she had to allow that it concerned . . . even rocked her. Had she misjudged him? In his place would she have been any more willing to let *him* go? Probably not. Then to what would she have stooped to get him to stay? Robbing his mailbox?

It was, she thought, the least she could have done. For Traders. For herself.

"But what I think," he added in a soft drawl, "doesn't matter. What you think is best for you—what you want to do with your life, Juniper—is what counts."

She breathed heavily. "Don't go human on me now, Gilliam."

He gave her a small smile, but that thrill of the challenge came into his pale eyes. "I haven't finished. I also realized, you see, that what's best for Killibrew Traders is no concern of yours."

She lifted her feet to a small stool and stared at them. "Of course you're right."

He dropped his hands to his sides, half turning away from her. "But you're curious, aren't you? You want to know what's going on at Traders."

She shrugged. "That's only natural, isn't it?"

"It's doing fine," he said, his words clipped, "just fine."

"Good." But was it? Cal was sorry, and Traders was doing fine without her. What more could she want? She raised her eyes to him. "Thanks for coming by, Cal."

He smiled, just slightly, but the warmth returned to his eyes. "You're welcome, Juniper."

"Are you going to tell me—really—why you came back?"

He took in a breath. "Because of you."

She'd had to ask, hadn't she? "I don't understand."

With a small laugh, he stepped in front of her so they were standing toe to toe, and cupped her chin. Very gently, rhythmically, he caressed her jawbone with his thumb. "Don't you?"

Their eyes locked. "Maybe I do." Aware of what she was doing, consequences considered and dismissed, she tucked her hand into his free one, feeling its warmth and strength. "We're so different," she said.

"I wonder if that's what draws us to each other."

She smiled, her eyes wandering over his face, taking in everything. He wasn't the stuff of dreams and fantasies. He was a man who belonged to this world, to reality. She liked that. She could feel her heart beating faster, and her smile deepening. "Who says I'm drawn to you, Gilliam?"

"Auntie Killibrew," he said, imitating Auntie's distinct Yankee accent.

Juniper laughed. "Auntie knows me well—but not that well."

"You're saying we're wrong?"

"Not necessarily." Her eyes took on a mischievous glint. "But Auntie thinks I'm hopelessly attracted to rogues . . . and I'm not sure you're such a big rogue, after all."

"You were this afternoon."

"But rogues never apologize."

His hand slipped down to her shoulder, fingers caressing her neck, sending sensations all through her. "They only swoop down upon the wronged damsel and force her to want what she is damned well convinced she doesn't want."

"Yes. Is that what you're trying to do?"

He didn't answer at once. "No."

"It would make sense, you know," she went on calmly, ignoring the sensations coming to life inside her. "You decide you want me. Reasoning I'm the type to be taken in by an apology, you come over and apologize. That way I decide you're not such a loathsome bastard, after all. You're at war with your baser instincts, unsure if going after me on behalf of Traders is worth alienating me. So your apology was insincere. Is that what you're saying?"

He looked amused. "Something like that."

She withdrew her hand, but his other hand remained lightly on her shoulder. "You stole my résumés because you thought my job hunting would give you leverage to lure me back to Traders—but afterward you felt guilty, didn't you?"

"Well . . ."

"Cal."

"Frankly, no."

She backed away, making his hand drop to his side. "What do you mean?"

"I was goading you, Juniper. You know that, don't you?"

"I suppose."

"It wasn't as much fun as I thought it would be. I wondered if the mailing was your way of goading *me*, but then afterwards I had to consider that you were actually, seriously in search of other employment. One part of me would do anything to get you back to Killibrew Traders—and if in the end you hated my guts, it wouldn't matter. But another part of me wants you to be happy, wants you to choose for yourself what's best for you. I apologized, Juniper, because I want to be your friend, not your enemy."

She regarded him skeptically. "Are we calling a truce?"

He grinned, grabbing her hand. "Probably not. I have a feeling we're destined to fight like hell half the time."

"And the other half?"

"Who knows?"

She let her hand slip up his arm, feeling the tough sinew of it...and the ache swelling inside her. It wasn't just physical. It was emotional, too. She had never thought there would be a place in her life for a man like this, and yet now she couldn't imagine his going away. But neither could she imagine his staying.

"Oh, Cal." She picked a stray cat hair off his upper arm. "I don't know what I'm doing up here—playing games, maybe. But I can't go back to Traders. I have my honor, for God's sake. I've been betrayed. It's all still so damned fresh...."

"Let's not talk about it anymore."

She smiled, her hand sliding up to his shoulder, and he eased his arm around her middle. They drew close. Nothing needed to be said. Without words, without any conscious signals, they came together, mouths touching, just once, and then again, briefly. But the hunger was too great, and Juniper's lips parted close to his, so he could feel her breath, and she could feel his. They came together once more, mouths open, tongues hot and exploring, the ache spreading, deepening, until she moaned softly and pressed herself against him, feeling his arousal.

He looked at her then. "Oh, hell."

"I know." She spoke with a smile.

"Do you want to go into the next room?"

"And damn the consequences?"

"I don't mean that—"

"I'm protected, for heaven's sake."

He grinned, kissing her lightly. "Savvy woman of incredible foresight that you are."

"Auntie's influence."

His brows went up. "Oh, really?"

She laughed. "Be prepared for any eventuality, she's always said."

"She's also told you to avoid rogues."

"If we continue to chitchat—"

"You'll change your mind?"

"No." She pressed her hand to his chest. "I'll melt."

"Point well taken," he said, his eyes twinkling. But suddenly they grew serious again. "You know what I mean by consequences?"

"I think I do."

"Do you want to talk more?"

"Do you?"

"I asked first."

"Frankly, no."

"Neither do I."

And they went into her bedroom. They left the shades up. The soft light of the moon and the stars shimmered on the glasslike waters of the Atlantic, and it seemed wrong to shut it out. They undressed silently. Juniper shivered in the cool night air, but then shuddered with warmth and anticipation when she caught the heat of Cal's gaze on her. He was still fully aroused, powerfully sensual in his nakedness.

"Should we blame fate?" he asked, coming to her.

She shook her head, feeling the swelling and tingling and aching spread throughout her body. "I think we have only ourselves to blame."

"Or congratulate."

She smiled. "Or congratulate."

He held her by the elbows, caressed them lightly, then circled her waist. She moved toward him, pressing her breasts against the wall of his muscular chest, and he moaned into her hair. Slowly he rubbed himself against her and slid his hands down her back, over the curve of her bottom, between her legs. She cried out softly, unable to remain standing, and they collapsed together on the bed.

"I've wanted you for so long," he whispered, lying on top of her.

She slipped her arms around the small of his back and felt the strength of him, the heat, the passion, melded it into herself. "I'm glad."

Cal dropped his mouth to hers then, kissing her languorously, filling her with longing. His mouth and tongue trailed down her throat to her breasts, where he slowly, gently licked each nipple until she moved beneath him, arching her hips, and pressed him hard against her.

"I want all of you, Cal . . . now."

She parted her thighs for him, and he came into her with a single, swift thrust that was so momentous, so beautiful and fulfilling that it was very nearly all she needed. He held still just long enough for her to catch her breath, and then they moved in unison, rocking, thrusting, feeling the sparks that had flown between them erupt into hot, blue-orange flames.

When it was over, they yelled together into the silent night. And sank into the soft sheets, listening to the waves pulse quietly onto the rocks. Even the wildest ocean storm couldn't have matched what had just transpired between them, Juniper thought, exulting in the light sheen of perspiration their bodies shared.

And Juniper dropped off to sleep, satisfied, still holding his warm, hard body to her.

She awoke sometime in the night and had to pull the sheet and blanket over her. There was no one with her anymore, and she wondered if it all might have been a dream. But she looked at the tangled bedsheets, and she still felt satiated by their long, hard, wondrous lovemaking. It hadn't been a dream. Yet sometime during the past few hours Cal had gone, slipping out into the night as coolly, silently and steadily as the ebbing tide.

8

JUNIPER WAS DUMPING coffee grounds in her herb patch outside the kitchen door, reliving last night, when a black BMW puttered down the dirt driveway and parked behind the pearl-gray Mercedes from Virginia. Summerfield drove a black BMW. Well, of course, she thought, springing to her feet. The cohorts!

She ignored the shaking of her fingers as she slammed back into her cottage. All last night—throughout his little apology and questionable explanations and exquisite lovemaking—Cal had to have known Summerfield was coming today. And he hadn't told her.

So what had last night been about? Hormones, she thought. Pure and simple.

"Once a snake," she muttered, letting the screen door smack hard behind her, "always a snake."

She, the astute and skeptical Juniper Killibrew, should not be lured by mere physical attraction. The sexual tension between them was undeniable, and she wasn't one to skirt the facts. But last night she'd begun to think she was falling in love with Cal, that she cared about him deeply, about his happiness, about his well-being. She was intrigued by his complexity, his sense of humor, his forthrightness. She sensed a broad range of emotions in him, some of them conflicting, all of them something she wanted to understand. Had the passion and sensitivity he'd exhibited last night been just another lie? A ploy? A tactic?

No, she decided. It hadn't.

"Maybe." She rinsed out her percolator. "Maybe not."

She fixed herself a tall glass of iced orange juice and headed out onto the terrace with Bo and the cats. At least they could be trusted.

"HEY, SUM." Cal opened the kitchen door. "What a surprise. What's up?"

Raking a hand through his hair and shaking his head, without a word Sum walked past Cal and plopped down at the table. In so many ways this older Killibrew reminded Cal of Juniper—not that he'd risk a host of new, unflattering names by telling her that. But he'd venture to guess she was more like her uncle and the rest of the Killibrew clan than she wanted to be.

Cal poured two mugs of coffee and sat opposite Sum. "Something's wrong."

Sum looked pained, and sighed. "Cal . . . you know I wouldn't interfere."

"Spit it out, Sum."

It's Juniper, Cal thought. After leaving her last night, he'd tossed and turned and cursed himself soundly and continuously for sneaking out on her. He wasn't sure why he'd done it. It had gotten so he could hardly think of anything else but her, them, what they could be together—and how it all could get torn apart. He hoped she had no regrets about last night. But no, Juniper wouldn't have committed herself to something she would have regretted in the morning.

Yet what must she be thinking now, with her uncle's car parked behind his? The morning fog had blown out to sea, the sun was sparkling on the bay, and here was the worried uncle out to warn the latest rogue off a Killibrew woman. What nonsense. In any case, it was a hell of a time for Sum, who had always declared that Juniper could take care of herself better than anyone else, to turn protective.

"It's Traders," Sum said.

Cal coughed in surprise. "What? Don't tell me you've decided you want back in?"

"No, no, it's not that." Sum shifted uneasily, fingering his coffee mug. He had the wild, tawny Killibrew hair quite unlike Juniper's and eyes a slightly deeper shade of gray than his niece's. But there was worry in them this morning, not the usual, carefree twinkle. "I thought maybe I should talk to Juniper—or try to. Cal, I was over at Traders yesterday. You were there yourself a few days ago. You must know what's going on.

"Arthur Green's a fine executive, Sum," Cal said coolly. *Damn.* Why did Sum have to bring up this mess? Cal wanted to talk about Juniper, not Killibrew Traders. Maybe, he thought, that was his problem. "Look, trust Green. He'll straighten things out. The company's going through a painful transition, that's all."

Sum shook his head. "Green's not Juniper, Cal."

"I know that." Cal immediately regretted the irritation in his tone. He drank some coffee, forcing himself to relax. "Sum—I can't force her back. She has a right to feel betrayed. If I weren't Cal Gilliam, the corporate raider, and you weren't Summerfield Killibrew, the uncle who didn't consult her about the sale—"

"I couldn't! It was difficult enough to go through with as it was. You don't know her."

"I'm afraid I do," Cal said dryly. "She'd have tied you up and locked you in a closet before she'd have let you sell Traders out from under her. But the point is, Sum, that she feels betrayed—and has every right to. She won't trust either of us. In her position, would you? And she's not coming back."

Sum gave his friend a long look. "Then why are you here?"

Cal managed a small smile. "It's never been easy for me to take no for an answer."

"You falling for her?"

"Sum—"

"I know you, Cal. She's not your type, but somehow I don't think that would matter. Juniper's a challenge to just about everyone she meets—and no one likes a challenge better than you." Sum sipped his coffee. Cal thought that would be the end of it, but then his friend said, "Well?"

"Maybe."

"Lord. Add more complications to this, why don't you?"

"Sum—"

"I know, I know. It's none of my bloody business. You and Juniper are adults, and I'm out of Traders, like I want to be. But, Cal, I hate to see the company hurt . . . or Juniper."

"I'm doing my best, Sum."

"I know. Juniper's not easy, is she?"

"No, but you gave me fair warning. Now what do you know about Traders?"

Sum shrugged, looking uncomfortable, perhaps even feeling a twinge of guilt. However well-planned and long-dreamed by himself, his exit had been abrupt and a surprise to everyone around him. All along Cal had wondered if his friend was playing his cards too close to his chest, but he'd decided that was none of his business. What did Cal care if Sum alienated his entire family? But that was before the vice president of marketing, the prickly Killibrew niece, had stomped into his life.

"Morale's low, Cal," Sum said. "Green runs the place—"

"Like Juniper would. He plays by the book. He's a rules man, Sum. You know that. I thought he'd be a good replacement for Juniper, hopefully a temporary one. Why do you think I hired him?"

Sum was looking dumb-founded. "You mean you— Good God, Cal, you think Green and Juniper have the same executive style?"

"Of course."

"This is all I need. Cal, Juniper's a *Killibrew*. She's never played by the rules in her life!"

Cal leaned forward, alert. "What are you saying?"

"She likes to pretend she's the only normal one in the family—God knows she's the only one of us who can get worked up about family tradition and classic clothes. She's a damned good executive. One of the best I've ever dealt with. But she's one of us, Cal. Just look at her. She has that godawful house in Portsmouth and those crazy animals, and when she quits her job, she sneaks up here to the middle of nowhere instead of getting her ass out and making contacts. If you tell her she has to skip, she'll jump. That's just the way she is."

"And her style?"

"Not by the book, Cal. *Nothing* like Arthur Green."

"Dammit. But she's so successful—"

"Because she works hard, knows her stuff, has faith in her staff and is willing to listen to new ideas and take risks. Don't let her fool you: she's a bottom-line woman. She just has her own ways of getting things done."

Like me, Cal thought unwillingly. *And like her uncle.* Of course she'd die before admitting to either comparison. Cal shook his head. "Then I've made a mistake."

"Get her back, Cal," Sum said gravely. "Do anything—but get her back. Or find yourself another Juniper Killibrew if you can. Green's kicking ass and taking names down there. If you don't do something, you're going to have an unholy mess on your hands."

Cal tensed. "I talked to him when I was down there, told him to go easy."

"Talk to him again. But it won't do any good; he doesn't know anything else. He'd be good at a Fortune 500 company, maybe, but not Killibrew Traders. We're—they're a bit different."

"I know, that's why I was interested in buying. Oh, hell." He sighed and looked at his friend. "Thanks for the warning, Sum."

"Yeah."

"You've got enough problems of your own. If you don't want to talk to Juniper, you don't have to."

"I don't mind. The worst she can do is use me as lobster bait." He smiled grimly, clapping Cal on the shoulder. "No, seriously, Cal, I don't mind talking to her—if it won't be counterproductive."

Cal nodded. "Frankly, I think it would be a help."

"Where is she?"

"This time of morning, she's probably out on the rocks composing her memoirs."

"Good. She'll have someplace to toss my body when she's finished with me."

It was only after he'd left that Cal decided Sum must have been kidding.

"WHERE JUNIPER KILLIBREW GOES, so goes her clipboard."

At the sound of her uncle's falsely cheerful voice, Juniper glanced behind her. She was sitting out on the rocks, not doing much of anything. Summerfield jumped over a crevice and dropped down beside her. To her surprise, he seemed tired and on edge—as if he'd been working, which, of course, was highly unlikely. He'd just made a fortune selling Killibrew Traders. Why would he work?

But in spite of everything, she was glad to see him. She usually was. Summerfield had that kind of effect on people—not his fault, she supposed.

"Hello, Summerfield." She smiled, squinting in the bright morning sun, for the moment forgetting Cal's treachery. "What are you doing here?"

"I wanted to talk to you."

"Seems to me you wanted to talk to your buddy Cal."

"Yeah, I wanted to talk to him, too."

"About what?"

"About stuff. June—" He broke off, looking away from her, out at the bay. "There was no need for you to quit. I thought— Well, I knew you'd be mad, but I thought you'd get over it and have enough sense not to cut off your nose to spite your face."

"I was mad enough to quit, Summerfield."

"That's the Killibrew in you." Again he stopped himself, looking at her now, his face filled with an anguish she didn't understand and certainly hadn't expected. "I want you to understand, June. I didn't do this to hurt you."

"You did it to make a nice profit and get yourself out of ever having to work again." Immediately she regretted the nastiness of her comment, and sighed, shaking her head. "I'm sorry, Summerfield. I'm sure you have your reasons, even if you choose not to articulate them to me."

He hesitated. "June—June, Killibrew Traders has always seemed more like your company than mine. It still is, no matter who owns the majority of stock. Cal Gilliam or me, what's the difference? You've never been one to care about blood and all that nonsense. Look, I sold out because I've never been interested in Traders the way I wanted to be. I've wanted for the longest time to make my own mark—but I never wanted to hurt you."

She looked at him closely. "Summerfield, are you telling me you're going into business for yourself?"

"That's neither here nor there," he said quickly, worrying her even more. "The point is that both Auntie and I think you should reconsider your resignation, for your sake *and* the sake of the company." He shook his head, more sad than impatient. "June, this isn't your style, being such an incredible dumb ass."

"Summerfield." She appraised him with narrowed eyes—uncle, traitor, friend, Killibrew. Damn Summerfield. Her life was always easier when he was elsewhere. "Is this a ploy? Are you part of Cal's plot to get me back to Traders? He put you up to this."

"No." He glared at her, exasperated. "You can be absolutely impossible. Stubborn. Juniper, it was a business decision to sell Traders and a business decision for Cal to buy it."

"And it wasn't a business decision for me to leave?"

"No."

"Maybe you're wrong. Maybe I've been waiting for a way out for years. I've been working my life away, Summerfield."

He stared at her for a moment, as if he just might believe her, then laughed bitterly. "Not a chance."

She shrugged.

"You're unreasonable, you know, June.

"Always have been."

He bit off something that sounded like a sigh of pure annoyance—another surprise. Where Juniper was concerned, Summerfield usually had an enormously long fuse. "Maybe Traders *doesn't* need you," he said. "Maybe this Arthur Green will do a damn fine job without you."

"It's possible, but I doubt it. I know Green, by reputation, at least. Cal made a mistake in bringing him in."

Summerfield began turning red. "Because he was desperate, for God's sake! You didn't leave him any room to maneuver, cutting out the way you did. What choice did he have?"

She turned on him. "What choice did *I* have? You didn't leave me much room to maneuver, either, Summerfield, sneaking around behind my back and selling Traders the way you did."

"Put it behind you, Juniper," he said softly, suddenly deflated. He touched her shoulder; she didn't pull away. "You belong in Portsmouth with Traders."

"And Gilliam? What am I supposed to do about him?"

"Maybe you belong with him, too."

WHILE JUNIPER WAS ON THE PHONE with a new, offbeat catalog company based in Houston, she heard Summerfield's car putter out the driveway. She refused to think about where he was going or what Cal intended to do now. Instead she concentrated on her conversation. The Houston catalog was one of the funniest and most original Juniper had ever seen, and its funky clothes weren't in direct competition with Traders' classics. She could move there with a clear conscience. The president had heard about the sale of Killibrew Traders, and he wanted to meet Juniper. They agreed on a date at the end of July, when she would fly down to Houston.

Once she got off the phone, Juniper tried to imagine herself in bright-turquoise leggings and orange sunglasses. Maybe she would feel obligated to wear company clothes.

She went out onto her terrace. Down on the rocks to her right, Cal was dragging a canoe toward the water. It was low tide, quiet and clear on the bay, a crisp morning perfect for canoeing. Juniper couldn't resist. She wandered over. The sun was glinting on his dark hair, and he wore khaki safari shorts and a white T-shirt that could, in fact, have been from a Traders catalogue but wasn't. Mostly she noticed the muscles in his bronzed legs, could almost feel them brushing up against hers. She herself was in Killibrew Traders walking shorts and a short-sleeved teal cotton sweater.

"Morning," she said.

He grinned at her. "You look bright-eyed and raring to go. Been working?"

"More or less." This, she felt, was no time to bring up Houston.

"On the memoirs or job hunting?"

"I'm writing a chapter on Grandpa Killibrew." Actually she'd jotted a note to Auntie suggesting *she* write the chapter on her missing brother. It was a start.

"I see. Would you like to take a break? There's another paddle up at the cottage. We can canoe around the peninsula, have breakfast somewhere and canoe back."

Breakfast? She'd eaten breakfast hours ago. Still, the idea of being out on the water was irresistible. She fetched the paddle, and they set off, Cal in the stern. He proved to be strong and skilled at maneuvering the canoe, and they stayed close to shore, where the water was calm and the danger of capsizing in the icy waters minimal. And the views, of course, were spectacular.

They hardly spoke at all. It didn't seem to be necessary.

Two peninsulas down and almost two hours later, they dragged the canoe ashore at a tiny restaurant that sat on stilts in the shallows. Inside there was just one not-so-big room. The walls were rough boards with insulation poking through the cracks, and there was a potbelly stove in a corner and a few tables scattered around, overlooking the bay. The food was cheap and plentiful and good, and the service was friendly. It was one of Juniper's favorite places.

"Great place to relax," Cal said, watching a duck and a goose paddle around in the shallows.

As she looked at him, Juniper saw for the first time that he was relaxed. She had thought, even that first day at the tulip festival, that Calvin Gilliam was a man never too far from having his feet up. And yet now she could contrast him with the individual at the festival, at the meeting announcing the sale, at her house afterward. He hadn't been tightly wound then—someone like him was *never* tightly wound—but more watchful, even on his guard. Perhaps he'd simply been ready for anything at all to happen. Now, however, after canoeing and breathing the ocean air, he seemed more open, more at ease—not so much ready for anything as simply ready to laugh.

They ordered homemade soup and something called fishburgers. Cal had vowed to come back and try their blueberry pancakes, but even he had to admit it was a bit late for breakfast.

"Has it been a while since you had a vacation?" Juniper asked.

"I thought, according to you, my whole life's a vacation."

She shrugged. "Pirating away companies may be fun for you, but it can't be very relaxing."

"Neither can working your ass off to cover for an uncle who never wanted to be the sole owner of a clothing company in the first place." He spoke matter-of-factly as he buttered a homemade biscuit. "Can it?"

"Depends," she said vaguely, refusing to elaborate.

"We both deserve this," Cal said, and with a single look, indicated everything—the rustic restaurant, the salt air, the ocean, the canoeing, the being together.

Their burgers and soup arrived, hot and steaming, the fish obviously fresh, lightly fried. "Decadent," Juniper said with a grin, and dug in. She was famished. The waitress refilled their coffee mugs.

A sudden rush of heat coursed through her as she realized Cal was watching her through narrowed eyes, his look intent. Sexual tension crackled between them. One night together had only made her want him more. She smiled breathlessly. "So . . . how was your visit with Summerfield? Did he say what he was up to?" She spoke rapidly, trying to control the sense of burning up. Even her fingers tingled. "I wonder what he plans to do with all his money."

"Why don't you ask him?"

"Me?" She laughed. "Perish the thought. I guess it's none of my business."

"He's your uncle."

"Don't remind me." She gave Cal an appraising look. "You're not going to tell me, are you?"

"It's not my place, Juniper."

"A rogue with a sense of honor," she said lightly, but was pleased. She appreciated people who could keep confidences. "Well, Summerfield can do as he likes. If he doesn't blow every penny, he'll probably invest in some wild scheme and lose everything."

"Are you worried?"

"No."

Cal smiled tenderly. "You are."

"I suppose where Summerfield's concerned, there's always room for concern. But he knows where I am. If he wants my advice, he'll ask for it."

"You think you're so different from the rest of your family, don't you?"

She looked at him in surprise. "Well, of course I am. You of all people must realize that. How could I get anything done if I were like them?"

"You tell me." He leaned back, watching her thoughtfully.

"What do you mean?"

Lifting his broad shoulders slightly, he peppered his soup. "I got Arthur Green to come in because he plays by the book—like you supposedly do. But apparently you don't and never did. I've found out, Juniper Killibrew, that you're as unorthodox as any of your eccentric clan. You—"

She tossed her head indignantly. "I'm not."

"Then prove it."

A challenge. "By going back to Killibrew Traders?"

"No." But his smile was downright devilish. "I promised my family I'd show up for the annual Fourth of July family picnic. Come with me. If you're so damned proper, you'll fit right in. You'll adore them, and they'll adore you."

"Is this a dare or an invitation?"

The smile broadened. "Both."

9

VIRGINIA WAS VERY HOT, very muggy and very beautiful. The Gilliams owned a hundred rolling acres in the eastern part of the state, in horse country. The Gilliams, of course, had horses. And white fences. And graceful oaks flanking a cobblestone drive. And a picturesque Greek Revival house, white with columns and a second-floor balcony. There were flower gardens of every variety, a herb garden outside the kitchen, a pool house and a stone stable.

This Juniper gathered merely from the circuitous drive onto the grounds and the conversation with Charles, Cal's younger brother, who had picked them up at the airport. Charles was more classically good-looking, certainly more proper and without a doubt more polite than his older brother. He called Juniper "Miss Killibrew" until she told him Juniper was fine, and even then he didn't look at all disconcerted. She might have been a Sally or a Buffy. She decided right away she liked Charles.

Cal had merely taken his younger brother's hand briefly and said hello, it had been a while. He let Juniper sit up front with Charles and didn't contribute to their conversation on the view, the neighbors, the state of the Gilliam gardens or what was in store for the weekend.

"Your brother's marvelous," she whispered to Cal as she climbed out of the car, now parked in front of a gate laden with sweet-smelling roses.

Cal glanced down at her, his expression unreadable. "I suspected you'd say something like that."

"I don't like your smug tone, Gilliam."

"My brother's what your Auntie would call a gentleman, isn't he?"

"Yes."

"Then I don't have to worry, do I? The Killibrew women go for rogues."

The smug tone remained, and Juniper shot ahead of him up the path. The stately house reminded her of her rambling Victorian, minus the weed-choked yard and the orange front door. That house was all that could be called the Killibrew spread, the family home, such as it was. Grandpa Killibrew, if still alive, was probably living in a grass hut. Her parents lived on a boat. Auntie had her little house in Portsmouth, purchased years ago with the money earned from her teaching. Sage lived in lodges and tents. Summerfield—one simply never knew where Summerfield lived.

No, she thought, the Killibrews weren't anything at all like the Gilliams. Carrying her bag, she walked slowly along the brick path to the front door. Here, family tradition *mattered*.

To everyone except Cal. In that regard, she had to admit, he fitted in better with the Killibrews—excepting herself, of course. Maybe that was it; they should switch families.

Ann Gilliam greeted them at the door, and Cal introduced his mother, a reserved, trim woman, striking but not beautiful. She seemed truly pleased to see her elder son and held out her hand graciously to Juniper, whom Cal had introduced as "the former vice president of marketing for Killibrew Traders."

"One of my favorite catalogs," Ann said. "I have a wool blazer from Traders that I've worn for *years*."

Juniper smiled. "Time to trade it in on a new one, perhaps?"

"Ah, the true saleswoman," Ann said, laughing.

One for Cal, Juniper thought, too late. In a low voice he said, "Old habits die hard."

Juniper ignored him. She didn't know whether fitting in with his family would disarm him—or reload his guns.

Ann instructed Cal as to which rooms they should use and left him to show Juniper upstairs. He leaped up the curved stairs two at a time. Juniper followed at a more discreet pace. She tried to ignore the movement of his long legs and slim hips, but that was difficult, and she found herself feeling that familiar ache inside her.

He waited for her on the landing. "It's a lovely home," she said, coming up beside him. The house was furnished in period pieces and yet managed to look welcoming and approachable—lived in. "I can hardly imagine you growing up here."

He smiled. "Mother's decorated over all evidence of her children's shortcomings."

"Meaning?"

"Meaning she wallpapered over the picture I drew of my horse on the living-room wall."

"Did she? My parents for years left my first sketches of a new fall catalog on the dining-room wall. They were amused—reminded them of my childhood, they said. I finally prevailed on them to paint over them when I was thirteen or so. It got to be embarrassing."

Cal was staring at her. "You drew sketches of a catalog?"

"The cover, yes."

"How old were you?"

"I don't know—four or five, I suppose."

He laughed in disbelief.

"So I was precocious. You have to understand, I've always lived and breathed Killibrew Traders. I—" She stopped herself, some inner alarm going off before she could dig her hole any deeper. "Of course, one does grow up. Things do change."

"They do," he replied, no longer laughing.

Her room, blue and white and cheerful, with a view of the side gardens, adjoined his, where she had no intention of venturing. They would share the bathroom at the end of the hall. Cal left her to get settled, which she did by flopping down on the four-poster bed and cursing herself for ever having let him lure her into coming. What had gotten into her? More to the point, what had gotten into to him? What was he up to?

Because he was definitely up to something. He always was.

Ten minutes later, he rapped on her door and walked in a half second before she said he could. "I thought I'd go riding before dinner. Care to join me?"

She was sitting on the edge of the bed. "No, thank you. I don't ride."

"No?"

"I've never made the time to learn."

"Sum does. I just assumed you—"

"There's not much that Summerfield does that I do."

"You're always too busy selling wool jackets and sketching covers."

He was so . . . impossible to ignore. So relentless and perceptive, and so very striking. She gave him a measured look. "I've always been committed to my work."

"What about yourself?"

"It amounts to the same." She rose to her feet and pulled back a curtain, looking down at the roses blooming below. "I have to meet my own standards of conduct, not yours or anyone else's. Have fun riding, Cal."

"I'd be happy to teach you."

"No." She was steady but firm, her mind conjuring up what an afternoon being coached by Cal in the art of riding would involve. Being physically close, for certain. Touching, at a guess. Perspiration, given the summer heat. No, it wasn't anything she needed to subject herself to right now. "I'd like to rest. Perhaps later I'll take a walk."

"Whatever suits you," he said quietly. "But Juniper—"

"Please."

He stood close to her, and although they weren't touching, her body reacted just as if they were. Even her skin grew hypersensitive. She listened to him take in a breath and expel it, slowly. Tensed and aching, she held on to the curtain and tried to concentrate on the roses. They were red.

"Perhaps later," he said, "we can take a walk together."

Juniper felt rather than heard him leave. She continued to gaze out the window as she listened to his footsteps in the hall, and she asked herself what she was doing here. Perhaps she should just catch the next plane out and travel the South Pacific with her parents for a few months. By her standards, that wouldn't be any farther away from who and what she was than spending the weekend in the Gilliam home in eastern Virginia.

BY THE TIME the family gathered in the living room for cocktails, Juniper had restored her sense of balance. Cal was the problem, she'd decided, not the Gilliams, not Virginia. He had gotten involved with the horses, leaving her to walk alone, and the fresh air had helped her gain a perspective on what was happening. Obviously Cal was going to twist her every comment to mean she should stay at Killibrew Traders. His invitation to Virginia was nothing more than the latest ploy in his strategy to return her to the vice presidency of his newest company.

Of course, it wouldn't work. She wasn't going back.

Arthur Green must be making a mess of things, she'd decided, not certain whether she should feel glee or consternation.

It's not my problem now, she told herself, smiling as she greeted Cal's sister, Marilyn. She proved friendly and brisk and very intelligent, and Juniper liked her at once. They had wine and ignored Cal, who, Juniper thought, seemed more amused than distressed by her behavior. This irritated her; she didn't want to amuse him. Nevertheless, she sat in a circle with Marilyn and Charles and their gray-haired, good-looking father, Robert, and discussed business. It was refreshing.

Cal refilled their wineglasses and talked horses with his mother, a well-regarded horsewoman.

Shortly before dinner, Marilyn's husband, Stephen, arrived after having stopped to check on their two daughters, who would be attending the picnic the following day. Stephen greeted Cal warmly, then joined the circle to discuss interest rates and the Federal Reserve. Once Stephen mentioned their children, however, the conversation digressed, and Juniper found herself trying to imagine Cal as the father of a couple of preschoolers—and found that she could.

To her relief, dinner was finally announced, but then Cal joined her, making it very apparent whom he intended to sit beside. "Having fun?" he asked mildly.

She nodded. "Your brother and sister are fascinating. They're nothing like you, are they?"

"Are you saying I'm not fascinating?" His voice was very low and deep and sexy, sending tiny vibrations down the length of her spine. He grazed her elbow, indicating she should follow him along the right side of the long table. "Actually, you're wrong," he went on. "*I'm* nothing like *them*."

"A small distinction," she said breathlessly, her voice nearly as low as his. She licked her lips, finding them dry and far too sensitive. Her mind was conjuring up images—feelings, memories—of his mouth on hers. Well, that just wouldn't do, as Auntie would say. She stood straight. "But you care about them. That's obvious, I think. And I suspect the biggest differences between you and them are on the surface—the ones that usually don't count a whole hell of a lot. On the inside, you're one of them. They know it, and so do you."

His eyes narrowed, his expression placid, unreadable. "I'm the black sheep, Juniper."

"Of course." She smiled. "None of you would have it any other way."

"Mmm."

"You know I'm right. It's impossible to—Cal, what's that look for? You're—dammit, you're *leering*. What did I say?"

"Not a word." He continued to leer; it was the only word for it: eyebrows arched ever so slightly, eyes fixed on her, mouth quirked in a half smile. Probably no one else in the room even noticed, but Juniper did. She realized she was meant to. He blinked twice. "You didn't say a thing, Juniper, rest assured."

"Then quit before someone notices—"

"Don't worry about that. I'm sure they've all drawn their own conclusions already."

"What? Here I am trying to have a serious conversation with you, and all you can think about . . ." She exhaled, growing exasperated with him and her situation. So much for her regained sense of balance and her new perspective! And suddenly there was something she had to know. She adjusted the skirt of her silk dress and dropped her voice to a whisper. "Cal, that night we spent together—it wasn't a fluke, was it?"

His smile broadened as he tipped the last of his wine into his mouth. "Not in the least. In fact, I think about it every time I look at you. We're going to have lots of nights together, Juniper. Lots."

LATER, in her room after dinner, she decided he'd done it on purpose—the remarks, the leer. He had wanted her to sit there at dinner thinking about when and where and how they were going to make love again. Fortunately, she was a master of deception and hadn't let on that she was even a trifle ill at ease. It was her marketing background, she told herself. She had smiled and conversed and asked for the rolls as if she'd been invited to Virginia by the entire Gilliam family and was their friend, not just Cal's.

Once Cal had brushed up against her knee, just to annoy her, even distract her. It was another ploy doomed to failure. She was one-track-mind Juniper Killibrew.

But now, alone in her spacious room, she could let her mind wander. In fact, she was so exhausted that she had virtually no control over what track it chose to take . . . and, naturally, it was a distressing one. As she lay on her silk sheets staring up at the ceiling, she found herself wishing the suspicions of the other Gilliams had been on target. That she and Cal were lovers, not enemies, not partners in business, not adversaries, not even friends. But lovers. In the physical sense.

She groaned. "Killibrew, there's no hope for you!"

As she rolled over and closed her eyes, willing him from her mind, she heard a movement in the next room. She hugged her extra pillow. If only he weren't so close. *You should have stayed in Maine* . . .

But a challenge was a challenge, wasn't it?

She flopped onto her back. She would *never* get to sleep!

She heard the bedsprings in the next room creak. She gripped the pillow and, just to calm her aching insides, pretended Cal was there in her room, in her bed, beside her. Black sheep and rogue and cohort of Summerfield Killibrew or not, he was impossible to get off her mind.

THE CATERERS ARRIVED EARLY the next morning, and
Cal, in shorts and a T-shirt, went out to help them set
up tables. He'd passed another in a long series of bad
nights, beginning with the day he'd met Juniper Killibrew. Although he'd been trying to unsettle her with his
remarks about what his family thought, he'd ended up
unsettling himself. They *did* think he and Juniper were
lovers. More to the point, they seemed to like the idea.
Today if any of them told him what a lovely, interesting, intelligent, warm, lively, witty, attractive person
Juniper was...

He swore to himself. Dammit, she did fit right in with
them. Why shouldn't they like her? She was exactly
what they'd always hoped for him.

"They don't know about her orange door," he muttered to himself. "They don't know about the cats and
the dog and the peeling wallpaper. She's a Killibrew!
Don't they know that?"

Didn't she know that?

He spotted her across the backyard, picking daisies
and petunias. Her hair shone in the morning sun. Cal
set up one last table and went to her. It was just as impossible to resist her here as it was in New Hampshire,
in Maine, or, he supposed, anywhere at all.

She wore a lightweight cotton camisole top and green
shorts, both, he thought, from some Killibrew Traders
catalog of the recent past. He didn't care about that. He
cared about the firm, lightly tanned skin of her arms
and the soft swell of her breasts and the toned muscles
of her long legs.

He inhaled deeply as he squatted down beside her.
"Enjoying yourself?"

She didn't so much as glance at him as she plucked another daisy, adding it to the bouquet in her left hand. "Trying."

"I suppose my family isn't exactly what you're used to."

"Not exactly." She dropped onto her knees and reached for another flower.

"They give Sum claustrophobia," Cal said. "You?"

She picked the elusive daisy, tucked it among the others and shifted her position away from him. She still hadn't looked at him. "If they're nice enough to have me as a guest, I'm not likely to complain."

Cal winced. "That's something my mother would say—or Marilyn or Charles."

"Your mother's a lovely person. So are your brother and sister."

Cal grunted. He loved his parents and siblings, to be sure, but he wasn't at all certain how he felt about Juniper liking them. Fitting in. How many times had he warned himself she would? That she wasn't his type?

She arched a glance at him, and, to his surprise, he saw that her gray eyes were glinting with mischief. "Just because I'm a Killibrew," she said, "doesn't mean I can't be civilized."

He rose, plucking a handful of daisies and handing them to her. "I can't figure you out."

Continuing to look at him, she smiled. "You don't have to."

"Playing hard to get? Not your style, I would think."

"Cal, I'm impossible to get—on any level. I won't go back to Killibrew Traders, and I won't— Well, let's just put it this way: you and I are as friendly right now as we're ever going to get."

"I look upon that as a challenge," he said, and walked off just as her airy smile faded and the glint in her eye turned to rage . . . and regret. This time, glib Juniper Killibrew had misspoken. Cal chuckled to himself. What the hell, he thought. She *was* a challenge.

He busied himself helping the caterers and ignored Juniper when she arranged her flowers in little glasses and set them in the middle of each table. His mother was delighted. Juniper accepted the praise with a sweet smile and a demure, "Oh, it was nothing."

Disgusted, Cal wondered what they all would think of the wiseass marketing whiz who'd threatened to dump mucky water on him. He felt like going over and kissing her—*that* would wipe that sickly-sweet smile off her face!

But what would a kiss do to *him*? He should have raided her room last night he realized, and been done with it.

He went inside and helped snap beans.

By noon, friends and family began to arrive, and Cal, swallowing his annoyance at Juniper, greeted everyone individually. He shook hands and asked polite questions, and when he saw Juniper standing idly next to an empty table, grabbed her and introduced her. He said simply, "This is Juniper Killibrew of Portsmouth, New Hampshire." She—or they—could supply the details.

Naturally she did. While he was chatting with an elderly second cousin, he heard Juniper inform a banking colleague of his sister's that she was the former vice president of Killibrew Traders. The banker said, "Yes, of course—Cal's new company."

He turned just in time to see her face darken. "Yes."

"Did you leave before Cal came along? Company was in pretty bad shape, was it?"

She grew rigid. "Last year Killibrew Traders profits jumped by more than a third."

"I see. Then—"

"I left for personal reasons."

Cal was positive only he could detect the venom in the glance she shot at him.

The banker rubbed his chin. "Well...I, er, excuse me, I should say hello to Marilyn."

Cal extricated himself from his conversation and started off quickly away from Juniper. She caught up with him. "Quit snickering," she said.

He looked at her, and had to inhale deeply, so struck was he by the life and energy he saw in those gray eyes. "Me?" he said innocently. "I wasn't snickering."

"You were. You *knew* I'd be in an awkward position here—"

"But you're masterly at handling awkward positions, aren't you? And I don't think you looked the least bit uncomfortable. You were mad, Juniper. Plain old hopping mad." He gave her a mild look. "It still grates, doesn't it? Not being with Killibrew Traders."

"It will *always* grate, but I'll go on."

"You're a survivor."

"Absolutely."

He grinned. "A true Killibrew."

That drew more venom from those lively eyes.

Cal shrugged as he made his way to the bar set up in one corner of the wide lawn. It was a magnificent day; not too hot, not too humid. He ordered two gin and tonics and handed her one. "Just tell people you're still with Traders," he said. "It'll be easier on you than having to explain."

"Easier on you, you mean. People won't find out what a heel you are."

"I'm afraid that's no secret around here," he said dryly.

"It doesn't matter. I don't lie."

More banking colleagues and extended family came by, and he smiled and said hello and made small talk. For no reason at all, he introduced Juniper this time as a friend of his from New Hampshire. Instead of interrogating her, they left her alone with him. A subtle use of words, he thought, but it worked.

Juniper didn't thank him. She said, "And since when have you become so damned proper and polite?"

"I beg your pardon?"

"There. You see? 'I beg your pardon.' Proper, proper, proper. You fit right in with the Gilliams. When push comes to shove, Cal, you're one of them. Black sheep my—"

"Juniper."

"I think I'll go mingle, *Mr. Gilliam*."

She stalked off. Cal sighed in utter confusion. If he was nice he was accused of being like his family. If he was nasty he was accused of being a rogue and God only knew what else. "Dammit, I can't win!"

So why was he watching her make her way through the crowd? Why was he waiting, breathless, for her smile? Why did he feel so extra *alive* when he was near her?

He liked the energy between them, he suddenly realized, but not the anger. Something in her anger—in the intensity of her expression, in her labored breathing—something made him want just to stop. To leave her alone. To let her find her own way. He cared about her. He wanted her to be happy.

Which she couldn't be with him pestering her about returning to Traders. To hell with that miserable company! If only he'd met Sum's prickly niece before agreeing to his friend's crazy scheme.

Against his better judgment—he was not a masochist—he joined Juniper at the edge of the lawns, where the children were playing Frisbee. She was watching, standing alone. He gently touched her arm. "You don't have to answer any questions, you know. You don't owe these people anything."

She sighed, her anger dissipating. He liked that about her; she didn't stew. "I know."

"I didn't expect this to be so awkward—"

"No sympathy, Cal, please. I'm as much to blame as you are. I like your family, and I'm sure most of their friends are just as nice as they are. If the situation with Traders was resolved, I'm sure I wouldn't feel so on edge."

He couldn't resist. "I thought it was resolved."

Her eyes flashed. "It won't be resolved until I find another position and you quit—dammit, just quit trying to seduce me into going back!"

"Getting you back to Traders has nothing to do with it," he said, gently, seductively rubbing her arm. "I want you, anyway, no matter what."

"Cal." Her tone was admonishing, but her eyes lit up, and then, slowly, the smile came. "You're impossible," she said with a laugh.

They walked together to the line at the buffet and afterward danced and played softball and laughed and joined in the festivities. She fitted in, Cal thought. And so did he. And then he thought, *with Juniper, anywhere is home.* Whenever he looked at her, whenever he touched her, inadvertently or intentionally, he felt the heat surge through him. He wanted her. And more and more he couldn't imagine life without her.

THAT NIGHT Juniper awoke in a sweat, disoriented, her heart pounding. Her sheets were in a tangle. Gulping for air, she slowly realized where she was . . . and that she'd been dreaming. About Cal. About touching him, wanting him.

"Good Lord."

She climbed out of bed, her knees still weak, and looked out the window, down at the rose garden in the pale light of predawn. She thought of the picnic. Had she ever laughed so hard? Had so much fun? Enjoyed being with anyone as much as she had enjoyed being with Cal?

No . . . no . . . no . . .

Below her, she saw the dark silhouette in the eerie light . . . a man. Cal. He was walking among the roses. He moved slowly, bending occasionally to smell a flower. She ached to go to him.

But she didn't . . . couldn't.

They would leave in the morning. She would redouble her efforts to find a new position, and then, finally, she would begin a new life. Nothing but anguish could result from continuing like this. She would lose sight of herself, become a part of him.

He was staring up at her window. She darted back out of his line of vision. How long had she been standing like that, thinking? She wasn't sure. Peering around the curtains, she noticed the flash of his teeth as he grinned.

Once a rogue, always a rogue. Auntie Killibrew had lived a long life, and some things she could be trusted to know.

Frustrated, Juniper exhaled loudly. Then why did she feel so warm and energetic knowing that Cal Gilliam wasn't just the sensitive, decent man she'd seen—and adored—at the picnic, but also the relentless individual she'd been dealing with since the tulip festival? He was an odd mix. And an intriguing one.

She went back to bed, but she wasn't even thinking about sleep when her door opened. She sat up, knowing, sensing it was Cal. He walked to the edge of her bed and leaned down. "How many sleepless nights will we cause each other before we figure out that we need to be together?" His voice was a tortured whisper. "Juniper, Juniper. I think about you all the time."

"We're a mess," she whispered back with a smile.

He kissed her then, his mouth already open, and she trailed her tongue across his lips and inside, probing, feeling the heat pour through her. She wanted to pull him down into the bed with her, undress him slowly and touch him everywhere and have him tell her over and over how much he wanted her, then show her, again and again.

But he pulled away abruptly and gave her a chaste kiss on the forehead. "If we were anywhere else," he said hoarsely.

She peered up at him in the darkness. "You're a Gilliam, after all, Cal."

He laughed shortly. "I guess I am."

She watched him leave, listened to him pad down the hall, and then rolled over and tried to quiet the stirrings in her body.

In the morning Charles drove them to the airport once more, and they headed north. To Juniper's relief, Cal didn't mention his predawn walk or where it had ended. Neither did she.

10

JUNIPER AND AUNTIE KILLIBREW were having iced tea at Juniper's cottage in Maine. From her own cottage on Mt. Desert Island, Auntie had brought a pot of geraniums, and she wore a matching red linen dress from a nineteen-fifties Killibrew Traders catalog.

"Juniper?" Her eyes narrowing suspiciously, Auntie eased herself into a metal chair on the terrace. It was a warm afternoon but misty. Auntie continued to scrutinize her great-niece. "You look rather terrible, Juniper."

Auntie had never been one to mince words. Debating her reply, Juniper poured tea from a large cut glass pitcher that she'd picked up for a song at one of Maine's ubiquitous flea markets. It was cinnamon herb tea, made by adding a half dozen tea bags or so to a jar of clear water and setting it out in the terrace in the sun for a few hours.

Juniper had also sliced a lemon—thinly, the way Auntie liked it—into a Depression glass bowl, and had made English-style cream scones.

Auntie was still peering at her, awaiting a reply.

"I'm sorry." Juniper smiled. "It's been an exhausting week."

"Is that so?" Auntie asked dubiously. "You haven't been working."

"Well, no, but . . . I've been to Virginia and back."

"Virginia?" The clear, alert eyes widened in momentary surprise, but the suspicion didn't dissipate. If anything, it increased. "Why on earth Virginia?"

"There was a party."

"I see."

Juniper shrugged, reaching for a lemon and squeezing it hard into her tea. She didn't want to talk about Cal, or even to think about him, which had become impossible.

Auntie paused. "You don't want to talk about it."

Leave it to Auntie, Juniper thought in relief, and although it wasn't a question, she smiled and said, "I guess I don't. I suppose we ought—"

"Juniper." Auntie reached for a scone and the jar of wild blueberry jam that Juniper always had ready when her relative came to visit. She slathered on some jam and sat back in her chair, holding the scone delicately between two sturdy fingers. "I noticed that the man who bought the company is staying at Summerfield's cottage. Calvin Gilliam, am I correct?"

Juniper frowned. Auntie knew damned well she was "correct." She'd changed tactics, Juniper realized, but not the subject. "Yes," she replied as noncommittally as she could. "I believe he's staying there. He and Summerfield are friends, you know."

"Yes, of course. But is he a nice man?"

What was that supposed to mean? Juniper shrugged, trying not to wriggle in her seat and give away her discomfort. "I suppose so."

Auntie grunted. "He didn't strike me as somebody who would worry about whether or not he was nice. How does he strike you?"

"Not as much of anything."

"Ah."

Obviously she'd made the wrong remark. But what would have been the right one? "He's a rogue, Auntie"? No, that wouldn't have done. "Auntie, please. Here, have another scone."

"I haven't finished this one. Do you miss Traders, Juniper?"

Questions, questions. Juniper silently chastised herself for not having realized Auntie had wangled the invitation to tea for exactly this purpose. Quitting Killibrew Traders and disappearing to Maine wasn't Juniper's style. Undoubtedly Auntie's interest had been piqued. Never underestimate a retired schoolteacher, she reminded herself. "Miss Traders?" Juniper laughed unconvincingly. "Hardly. It's been a delightful summer up here—so quiet, few disturbances. Really, I have the life."

"I don't believe you."

Juniper refused to cave in. "You'd be surprised how quickly one can get used to doing nothing."

"One, perhaps, but not you, Juniper."

While Juniper buttered a scone and tried to conceal her growing exasperation, Auntie Killibrew studied her great-niece with a mildly curious, somewhat knowing expression on her wrinkled face. She'd never been one to worry much about wrinkles and sags and such; she was herself and proud of all the years she'd lived, and people could take her as she was or be damned. In spite of her cantankerous attitude, or perhaps because of it, she had a multitude of friends. She truly cared about people. And especially about Juniper.

Knowing this, however, didn't lessen Juniper's frustration.

Auntie sipped her tea, stirred it, squeezed a lemon slice into it and finally regarded Juniper with pursed lips. It was her let's-get-to-the-point expression, the one feared by decades of recalcitrant students. "Juniper," she said, "you know I've never regretted not marrying."

Juniper coughed in surprise. "Well, of course."

"I've lived a full and contented life," Auntie went on. "Don't know what in blazes I'd have done with a man if I'd had one; probably would have just slowed me down. I've no complaints, only many things for which I'm eternally thankful."

This time Juniper knew better than to interrupt. Fortunately Auntie's lectures were infrequent, but when the mood struck her to pontificate, no one dared try to distract her from the point she was working up to making. And she always had a point.

The elderly woman rested her tea glass in her lap. "I'm happy with my life."

It was as if Juniper hadn't spoken. Shifting slightly, Auntie said, "But I can truthfully tell you I never let a man slip through my fingers just because I was too darned stubborn to admit I was falling in love with him."

"What? Auntie!" Juniper sputtered and jumped up. This was just too much. "Auntie, if you're saying what I think you're saying...well, you're wrong! Calvin Gilliam is...why, I'm no more in love with him than— than with a *slug*."

Settling back in her chair, Auntie smiled in amusement. For a moment she said nothing, letting Juniper's own outburst hang in the air for a while. But Auntie did love having the last word. "That's very good, Juniper," she said. "Excellent. It does say everything, doesn't it?"

"Auntie—"

"Juniper, Juniper. Please. Did I even mention Calvin Gilliam?"

"You didn't have to. You—" Juniper sighed and collapsed against her chair. "Victory to the old woman in the faded linen. All right, all right. Gilliam has his points, Auntie, I admit, but there's no hope of anything happening between us—nothing of permanence, anyway. And you know me. I'm not your—" She hesitated, wondering how she could phrase it delicately. "I'm not the type to get involved with someone knowing there's no hope for commitment. I just can't. It's not who I am. And it has *nothing* to do with being stubborn!"

Auntie reached over and with surprising strength grabbed her niece's wrist. "Who says there's no hope?"

"He owns Traders."

"Oh, nonsense, is that all? Heavens, you two could run that company together—"

"No!"

"My, we are stubborn, aren't we?"

"Just realistic. It's not just the company, Auntie. We're totally different people. We have different backgrounds, different interests, different ways of doing things."

"So? That should make life much more exciting."

Juniper exhaled loudly. "Oh, Auntie. Here, another scone?"

If there was one thing Auntie had learned in her seventy-plus years, it was when to drop a subject. "Of course. But just one more thing: I believe Summerfield has orchestrated his own fate, and you should give him that much credit. Whatever he is, he's *not* a victim of Calvin Gilliam."

They finished tea, and afterward, when Auntie had gone off to her own cottage, Juniper went inside and flipped through the summer Killibrew Traders catalog. She would need a new suit to wear to her interview in Houston. It was a minor consideration, but easier than trying to figure out what Auntie Killibrew knew that she wasn't telling her great-niece.

After she'd eaten her supper alone, with Bo and the cats angling for affection, Juniper walked out on the rocks. She found Cal on one of the farthest boulders on the point, just sitting there as the tide rolled in. Not even wanting to resist, she made her way over to him and sat down. "Good evening," she said.

He glanced at her and smiled briefly, but she saw immediately that his face was gray with fatigue, the fine lines in his forehead and at the corners of his eyes more pronounced. "Evening," he drawled.

"You look pretty worn out."

"Long day."

She tried to hide her surprise. Did Cal Gilliam have long days? "Even here?"

"Especially here."

She looked away.

"I didn't mean that," he said quietly, the sincerity in his deep, low voice drawing her back, easing her sense of discomfort. "I've been on the phone most of the day with Artie Green—and Sum. We've got problems, Juniper. Not you, of course. As you've made it damn clear, you're out of Killibrew Traders. But you're one hell of an act to follow, you know."

He had her interest now. What was happening at Traders? What had Artie Green done to her company? She asked as evenly as she could, "What do you mean?"

"Artie's not a good replacement for you. I made a mistake in asking him to act as interim vice president."

She shrugged. "I could have told you that."

"If I'd asked?"

She said nothing.

"I made a lot of assumptions, Juniper. About you, the company, your family. Some of them were on target but not all."

Their legs dangled off the boulder. Below them a wave crashed onto the rocks, covered with barnacles and snails. Cold salt water misted them, but it felt good. "That's all right," Juniper said. "I've made a lot of assumptions about you, too. What's done is done—"

"No." He cut her off, not raising his voice at all, and his gaze held hers. She noticed the softness of his eyes, the depth and honesty in them. This was Cal Gilliam at his most irresistible. He went on in that steady, quiet voice. "It's not over, Juniper. You can't run from your family, from who you are. You have to try to understand why Sum's done what he's done, to get him to explain it to you. You have to talk to him, Juniper. And me—you can't pretend I haven't bought Killibrew Traders. I have. I own the company."

"I haven't forgotten," she said coolly. "Not for a second."

"Haven't you? What about when we're together? What about when we're kissing, when you're thinking about making love with me? Juniper . . ."

"You're getting carried away with your own theory, Cal. I've never—"

He smiled, his eyes lighting up. "You've never thought about making love with me again?"

"I . . ."

"You're the one who doesn't like to lie. Tell me the truth now. Tell me it hasn't crossed your mind what we'd be like together the second time—and third and fourth."

"Well, for heaven's sake." She jerked away, looking out across the bay. The mist had settled in, obscuring the view of the offshore islands. "If we weren't stuck up here on a point all alone—I'm only human, you know."

She could feel his smile. "You've thought about us in bed from the first time you saw me at the tulip festival."

She whirled around, nearly losing her balance on the edge of the rock. "What makes you so sure?"

"It's what I was thinking."

As he edged closer his hard thigh rubbed up against her, and it was all she could do not to just throw herself down on the rocks in an open invitation. Lord, she thought, what an effect he had on her! And what tactics. He knew precisely what he was doing: getting her to admit, if only to herself, that she did think about making love with him, almost all the time. At night, in the cool light of morning, in the heat of the afternoon. Anytime, anywhere. The prospect of being with him, of loving him until the ache inside her was no more had begun to consume her thoughts, her energy.

And the more she thought about loving him, the more she yearned for it, the more she would force herself to remember who she was and what they had between them. She would tell herself, as she did now, that he was the Gilliam who had bought Killibrew Traders, and she was the Killibrew who had worked so hard to expand the company, had covered for her uncle for so long, and then had finally quit. Because of Cal Gilliam.

The crashing of the waves directly below them prevented her from hearing his breathing, but she could feel the warmth and freshness of it on her face, and she heard herself give a little gasp. It was becoming increasingly difficult to remind herself of all the reasons she shouldn't want him.

"You must have had a hard day," she said, attempting to sound lighthearted. Instead she sounded breathless, even to herself. And talking seemed only to make her lips more sensitive, tingling for the touch of his mouth.

"In some ways," he whispered.

"I wish I knew where all this would end."

Had she moved? She didn't know, but they were closer. Her heart was pounding, and her mouth was so near his. Her lips grazed his . . . or was it vice versa? It didn't matter. She let out a little sigh of pleasure at the feel of his mouth, so right, so achingly right. Her mouth opened, and she ran her tongue along his, feeling the heat of it, flicking hers against his teeth, reveling in the moan that escaped from deep inside him.

With one finger she trailed a path along the knot of muscle in his upper thigh, and slowly, torturously moved up along his hip. He grabbed her hand suddenly and pushed it against him so she could feel the strength of his arousal.

It was her turn to moan. "Cal . . ."

"Don't say anything," he whispered. "Not a word."

He shifted so that he was facing her and snatched her up by the waist, drawing her onto him. He raised her shirt. His hands were warm on her bare skin. She inhaled sharply, feeling her breasts swelling, her body throbbing for more of him, all of him.

"We shouldn't—there's too much unresolved."

His answer was to slip his fingers inside her bra, to send thousands of tiny shivers through her as he touched the sensitive peaks of her nipples.

Then he slid her back down to the rock. "I know," he said curtly, and jumped off the rock.

The breeze felt cold. She watched him walk down to where the tide was coming in. Carefully balancing himself, he stuck a bare foot into the frigid North Atlantic water. He grinned up at her. "It helps," he said, his ravaged features softened by the fading evening light. "You should try it."

She sighed, and after she'd climbed down onto the rocks, they both found places to sit among the barnacles. They rolled up their pant legs and hung their feet in a crevice between two boulders, letting them get drenched with the ebb and flow of the tide. The water was so cold their feet hurt and turned red. But it was exhilarating. To warm them afterward, they walked along the sun-heated rocks, holding hands.

We can be friends, Juniper thought. *We're civilized.*

But the ache of wanting him was still there, dulled only slightly by the icy tide, and it didn't help one bit knowing he felt the same.

He squeezed her hand. "Coffee?"

"I'll be up all night."

"Then by all means," he said, and laughed.

She grinned. "You're impossible."

"So are you."

"Maybe that's why we keep at each other."

His laugh turned into an easy smile as he swung her arm. "I suspect living with you's no picnic."

They were heading back to the cottage. "Bo seems to like it—"

"I'm no dog."

"And you're not living with me, either."

He looked at her, his expression only mildly serious, but the honesty, the sincerity were there in his eyes. "Not yet."

She decided not to take him seriously. "It's never been tried, you know. Somehow in my thirty years on this planet, I have managed to avoid really 'shacking up' with a man, as Auntie would call it. Not that I'm inexperienced in matters of the heart, you understand, but there's something to be said for living alone. And I suppose you guessed it. I'm no picnic to live with."

"Yup, I guessed it." He leaned toward her and said into her ear, "And I don't care."

THE WARMTH OF THE COFFEE did nothing to ease the tension that seemed to stretch every nerve in Juniper's body. They had to sit inside. Although it was a warm evening, the mosquitoes were swarming, thick, slow and profoundly irritating. They clung to the screens, along with a few dozen moths, and peered inside like voyeurs.

Cal didn't seem to notice. Stretched out on the couch, he balanced his mug on his flat stomach as he talked, blandly and without any indication of lingering arousal, about sailing.

Juniper sat perched on the edge of a tacky vinyl-covered chair, but she couldn't bring herself to concentrate on a single word Cal uttered. She didn't give a damn about sailing, not right now.

But she did care about how he was talking, about the delicious huskiness of his deep drawl, the placid expression on his striking face, the breathtaking paleness of his cornflower eyes. She could understand how Summerfield had been lured into selling Killibrew Traders to this fascinating rogue of a man. Why not? Calvin Gilliam had a persuasive personality.

"Juniper?" He raised himself slightly and looked at her, his thick eyebrows drawn together, at once stern and amused.

Juniper jumped, somewhat startled by his abrupt change in tone, and blinked. "Hmm?"

"You haven't been listening."

"I have . . . more or less."

"Bored?"

Hardly. But she only shook her head.

"Tired, then."

"Not at all. I was just—Cal, why do we always avoid the issue?"

He shrugged, sighing. "I suppose because the issue is a problem, and the problem seems insoluble."

Her shoulders sagged. "Killibrew Traders."

With one graceful and yet confident gesture, Cal set his mug on the coffee table and swung his legs down, planting his feet firmly on the floor, a part of their problem, Juniper realized. They were both people with their feet flat on the floor. In their own ways, practical. In their own ways, realists. It was a cliché, perhaps, but apt.

And at least it was something they had in common.

"Even if I hadn't bought Traders," he said gravely, "we would still be as drawn to each other as we are repelled by each other. We would still have our problems."

She smiled easily. "Repelled is a bit strong, isn't it? Makes me feel like a can of Raid—or a big, fat mosquito getting ready to bite your neck."

"Don't get us started again," he warned with a very dry, very pointed look.

"Mmm, yes, I understand what you mean. But what about infuriated? We're as drawn to each other as we are infuriated by each other. That works better, don't you think? You do infuriate me."

His eyes gleamed wickedly. "But I don't repel you?"

"Well…all right, look. You're Summerfield's friend, and despite your 'raider' reputation, hardly a man driven, and certainly not a man who plays by the rules or even knows them. I on the other hand—"

"Know all the rules and break them, regardless." He picked up his mug and blew at the hot coffee, his eyes resting ever so casually on her. "Right?"

She tossed her head airily. "But I've calculated and accepted the risks. *You* jump into murky water head first, without figuring out anything beforehand."

"So you're tedious and hardheaded."

"Decisive and fair."

He sipped his coffee. "There's no hope for us."

She grinned. "None whatsoever."

Again he set down his mug, then leaned back and eyed her closely. "So what do you say?"

"You mean do I want to spend the night, anyway?"

"That's exactly what I mean," he said quietly, in that slow drawl that turned her spine to hot liquid. "I don't give a damn what you are on paper—what you and I would look like on some damned computer dating screen. I know what I feel when I'm with you, and it's not what I've felt with anyone before in my life. Stay the night, Juniper."

She breathed deeply. "Will you sneak off afterward?"

"No."

He rose and carried his mug into the kitchen area, and Juniper watched the easy way he moved, the play of the solid muscles in his arms and long legs. Physically, he was a man of both grace and strength. It was a heady combination.

"What about you?" she asked softly. "Is this what you want?"

He half turned, smiling at her. "Yes. I've been rattling on about sailing when all I want to do is make love with you."

She nodded. "We're not just a set of characteristics, are we?"

He looked surprised. "I hope not. What has that got to do with anything?"

"I was just thinking. When you get to be thirty it's more difficult to put aside expectations. I've had more time to think about what I want and need in a relationship than if I'd committed myself to someone when I was twenty-one. I'm used to looking for certain characteristics, certain things I seem to need in a relationship."

"None of which I have?"

She laughed, unembarrassed. "Well, a few."

"Same goes for you, sweet cheeks."

"But a friend of mine, a family therapist, in fact, once told me that the mate you choose is the one who breaks down all those expectations. Maybe she had a point."

"Maybe."

She climbed to her feet. "Just one thing."

He looked at her. "What, Juniper?"

"Let's leave the shades up."

11

THEY STOOD, unclothed, looking out at the bay, listening to the waves and smiling at the stars and each other. "It's a beautiful night," Juniper said, warm and unselfconscious.

Cal slipped an arm around her waist. "It would be," he said in a low, husky voice, "even if it were storming outside."

The feel of his skin against hers brought only pleasure, a thousand kinds of pleasure, but no trepidation, no second thoughts, no private belief that this was crazy. This was right. Absolutely and incontrovertibly right. She belonged here tonight.

He had said she was beautiful, and so was he, so straight and brown and tall. "I love to look at you," she said.

He laughed softly. "I hope that's not all." And he touched his lips lightly to the flesh just below her ear.

She felt his breath warm on her face and turned into him as his tongue flicked against her cheek, and then into her mouth. Moaning with pleasure, she pressed her breasts against the hardness of his chest. She heard him catch his breath as his mouth opened wide, urging her to deepen the kiss. She obliged.

"You keep rubbing up against me like that, and we could have trouble," he said, slipping both his hands onto her hips.

"Good." She laughed and rubbed harder, feeling just how aroused he was, which increased her own longing. "I could just jump on you right now...."

He breathed deeply, achingly, at the very idea, and his hands slid down the curve of her bottom. "Care to try?" And he gripped her, pulling her up; automatically her thighs parted, and she straddled his hips.

He brought her down slowly, and she was more than ready as she felt him coming into her. They cried out together, clutching each other, savoring the moment.

But the longing was too much, too insistent, and she fell backward toward the bed, Cal keeping her from landing on her head, so that she tumbled instead onto the warm, threadbare quilt. It smelled of old attics and lazy summers and all that was right, so right, about being with someone you loved. Loved? Juniper smiled to herself. Wasn't that it? Wasn't that why she was here? Because she was in love with Cal Gilliam?

She smiled as he came to her, into her again immediately. Then he thrust deeply, and she could tell herself no more, and him nothing, except with her body. Over and over again, thrashing and loving and wanting, they let mind and body and spirit unite. It was their choice, their destiny.

And when it was over, when she again could hear the steady rhythm of the waves outside and smell the cool night air, she turned to Cal, stretched one arm over his broad back and smiled as she fell asleep.

JUNIPER AWOKE FIRST, with the sun ... and with no regrets. Stretching, she smiled at Cal, asleep on his back, peaceful, strong and sensual even in repose. She would never forget last night. Never. No matter what it led

to—or didn't—she would refuse ever to see their lovemaking as anything less than a beautiful, memorable
exchange.

She slipped soundlessly out of bed and put on one of
his shirts, one of deep-plum cotton, smelling of him,
and padded downstairs in her bare feet. It was a cool
morning, but the sun, shimmering on the bay, quickly
warmed the tiny cottage. She made a pot of coffee and
sat outside on the porch.

Perhaps things could work out between them. She
sighed, wondering. She kicked out her feet and hoisted
them onto the porch railing, coffee mug in her lap, the
fresh, brisk air in her lungs. "It's not your style to give
up," she told herself aloud. "You're not a quitter."

No. But neither was it her style to pursue what was
impossible, unattainable, futile.

Cal appeared at the screen door. He wore only a pair
of bikini underpants, dark blue, that showed about an
inch of white skin meeting the tan line below his navel.
Juniper had to catch her breath at the sight of him. Noticing, he smiled devilishly. "Aren't you glad I didn't
turn into a toad overnight? Morning, Juniper."

There it was again: the delicious drawl. No one could
say her name the way he did. She smiled over at him,
her feet still propped up on the rail. "Good morning,
Cal. There's coffee on the stove."

"In a minute. I was thinking about climbing mountains today. You?"

"Rhetorically speaking, yes."

His eyes narrowed slightly in thought, and his voice
dropped. "Yes, I know what you mean."

"But you were thinking about physical mountains,
am I right?"

"Mmm. I thought we could take a trip to Mt. Desert Island and pick a real mountain to climb."

"We could pack a picnic lunch."

He grinned wickedly. "There's more of Sum's peanut butter around here somewhere."

She flew to her feet, going after him, laughing, but he caught her up by the waist and swung her against his chest. And that was that. She curled her arms lazily around his neck and laughed into his mouth. "Rogue," she said, kissing him.

"I'll show you rogue," he said, laughing back at her.

Pirate style, he hauled her upstairs—and not for a second did she even consider protesting.

THEY SPENT THE NEXT DAYS together, picnicking, mountain climbing, walking along the shoreline, hunting for tide pools. They would sit out in front of their cottages for hours with binoculars, watching eagles and cormorants and even the occasional loon. They played Frisbee with Bo, and they let the cats curl up in their laps in the evening while they sat and read or just talked.

Sometimes they slept at his cottage. Sometimes they slept at hers.

Cal couldn't remember when he'd been more content. He never tired of being with Juniper, not in spite of her tenacity and argumentative nature, but because of it. He didn't have to pussyfoot around her. He could just say what was on his mind.

But there were mutually and tacitly agreed-upon subjects that were taboo: Killibrew Traders, Summerfield, memoirs, job hunting and the item on Juniper's calendar that said, "Houston, two p.m., Greenway Plaza."

All his life Cal had lived for the moment. Now his heart and mind kept urging him to consider what would happen tomorrow and the next day. He couldn't let Juniper slip away. They were right together.

At least when they were in Maine they were. There was no interference from the outside world, from family and work and responsibilities and duties. Here they could be anything they wanted to be, but they couldn't remain tucked away on this isolated point forever. Juniper had to get on with her career. And he had to make a decision about Killibrew Traders and who would replace the departed vice president of marketing.

On a hot, clear morning late in July, Artie Green called, catching Cal alone at his cottage, a rarity. "Cal," Artie said, his voice grave. "Cal, my bag of tricks is empty. I'll give you another week, but you're going to have to find somebody to run this company—or get your act together and come run it yourself."

"You know my expertise isn't in day-to-day operations."

"What I *know* is that Juniper Killibrew has been doing the work of three people. Cal, something has to be done."

"Great timing, Artie," Cal said, running his hand through his hair. "Look, can you recommend anyone? Anyone there I can move up?"

"You want my advice?"

"Hell, yes!"

Artie didn't hesitate a moment. "Get Juniper Killibrew back. She put her heart and soul and a hell of a lot of talent into this place, and people around here know it. Offer her the sun and the moon, Cal, but get her back."

Cal sighed bitterly. "What if she won't take the sun and the moon?"

"Lie. Coerce. Plead. Threaten. Cajole. Word is she's off writing her memoirs and half the catalog companies in the country are after her. Get to her first. Killibrew Traders needs her, Cal."

"Damn. The news could get worse, could it?"

"Wait till the quarterlies," Artie said grimly, and hung up.

Very nearly wishing he'd never laid eyes on Summerfield Killibrew, Cal headed over to Juniper's cottage. As had become his custom lately, he didn't bother knocking. But the moment he walked into her cozy living room he realized that this once he should have knocked.

Juniper stared at him sheepishly, caught. She was wearing something that resembled— Well, Cal didn't know what. It was much too loud even for a circus clown costume. He stared at the tight-fitting bright-turquoise leggings, the skinny orange top over which hung a monstrous button-up sweatshirt in one of the ugliest mixes of colors and geometric patterns he'd ever seen. Her hair was held off her face by a scarf that picked up two of the patterns in the sweatshirt. Something fierce and unapproachable hung from her ears. He blinked. Dragons, they were. *Dragons.* They were black and green and, apparently, earrings.

On her feet were black elf boots—at least, that was what they looked like—and she had on, at the minimum, three pairs of socks; one black pair, one orange

pair, and one a mix that matched the scarf . . . maybe.
He couldn't be sure.

"Maine must be getting to you," he said cautiously.

"It's my new look." She spun around, and he winced
at the kaleidoscope effect. "What do you think?"

It was positively horrendous, but he decided not to
say so. "New look for what?"

"For whatever."

If she wasn't lying, she was at least being evasive, but
Cal chose not to push her, nor to worry. Whatever else
he didn't know or understand about Juniper Killibrew,
he was absolutely confident that *this* wasn't her.

"You're rebelling against the classicism of Killibrew
Traders," he suggested. "Experimenting with new types
of clothing."

She shrugged. "Lots of people dress this way. It's very
popular."

"Not among marketing vice presidents, I should
think. Where did you get this stuff?"

"Ordered it."

More evasiveness. "On a whim?"

She grinned. "Not like me, is it? Maybe getting away
from Killibrew Traders has changed me. Maybe I'm
becoming more like Grandpa Killibrew and Summerfield—"

"Maybe you've always been like them, in your own
way," he interrupted quietly, walking over to her. If he
stood just so, the glare didn't bother him. "You're a risk-
taker, Juniper, and an adventurer—admit it."

She leaned back on her heels. "You know me so well,
huh?"

"Getting there."

"I could say the same about you, you know. You're not the lazy oaf you like to come across as being. You definitely have your own way of doing things, but that's my point: you *do* get things done."

He turned away, remembering Artie's call and feeling a stab of guilt and even shame—as well as frustration. Because of his feelings for Juniper and his own stubborn selfishness, he was letting his company go to hell. He *wasn't* getting things done. He had shirked his responsibilities, and maybe Juniper was right; that wasn't like him. In that way he was like the rest of his family.

Looking back at Juniper, he had to smile. She looked so alive and fresh and damned ridiculous in those clothes. How could he leave her now? He didn't want what they had to end. He wanted to prolong their life up here for as many days—weeks, months, years—as possible.

"You look awfully serious," she said.

"Do I?" He shoved thoughts of Artie aside and moved closer. "I was just wondering if you might want to change your clothes."

"Into what?"

He touched her chin. "Into nothing."

WARM AND SATIATED, Juniper gathered up the clothes she'd ordered from the Houston catalog company and returned them to the plastic bags they'd come in. She smiled as she plucked a sock from a lamp shade. How had that ended up there? Kissing her languorously, Cal had left; they would have dinner together later. Juniper was appreciative of the time alone. She needed to think.

Weird as they were, the clothes were well-made, promptly delivered, enticingly packaged. Of course, they would undoubtedly outlast the fad that had made them so popular, but at least customers were getting their money's worth in quality for the exorbitant prices. Killibrew Traders clothes were, by and large, timeless, hardly on the cutting edge of fashion.

That might be an interesting change, Juniper thought. Marketing fads. Could she do it? Well of course she could. That wasn't the question. The question was did she want to do it.

Sighing, she set the clothes inside her cedar chest, where they could die a natural death or wait until she remembered a friend or a teenager or someone who liked wild, funky clothes.

She supposed wanting to go to Houston—or not— had very little to do with anything, when it came right down to it. Houston would be a challenge, and if it didn't work out, there would be another catalog company somewhere.

And that, she thought miserably, was the point. In all her time with Cal, in all their soul-baring conversations, she had never been able to tell him about the scheduled interview in Houston. It was an intrusion of reality—a sometime, somewhere she didn't want to face.

What she wanted more than anything was for Maine to go on forever. But she knew it couldn't. The Houston interview was in less than a week.

12

JUNIPER GRITTED HER TEETH as she climbed the rocks on the way to Cal's place, which was how she thought of the little chalet now; somehow she'd managed to banish all thought of Summerfield. It was a damp, foggy afternoon, typical of the northeast coast. More than seeing it, she could hear and feel the ocean behind her. How appropriately bleak. Her appointment in Houston was two days away.

At her own cottage, Juniper had had a fire going, and she'd spent most of the day there alone. Without badgering her to explain her quiet mood, Cal had left early that morning, giving her the time and space she needed just to think. That was something she admired about him. He wasn't threatened by her need to be alone sometimes. And he trusted her.

"Poor, misguided soul that he is," she muttered under her breath, feeling even more like a snake in the grass. She had used her alone time to pack for Houston. Her plane tickets had arrived by mail, and she'd tucked them into the side pocket of her carry-on bag, a Killibrew Traders item that, she trusted, the Houston people would never even see. She had opted for the only non-Traders suit she owned, a pale-lemon linen.

Cal was inside, whistling a tune as he worked on some culinary masterpiece. It was his night to cook. They'd been alternating, and all that kept them from

gaining weight, Juniper was positive, were their endless hikes and endless nights of lovemaking. She hadn't
felt so trim and healthy in years.

He had a fire going too, and when he saw Juniper, he
grinned broadly. She ached all over. No matter what
happened, she would never feel for anyone what she felt
for him. The long days in Maine, with no schedules and
no battles to be dealt with or fought, had relaxed them
both. Perhaps, she thought, Cal shouldn't have let his
guard down.

But she couldn't resist wondering whether it was
Maine that had refreshed him or their relationship.
She'd noticed herself whistling more of late, too.

"What are you making?" she asked, hoisting herself
onto the counter next to him. She was in sweatpants
and sweatshirt, he in jeans and sweatshirt.

"Buttermilk biscuits," he said, kneading the soft,
white dough with his powerful hands. "To go with the
fried chicken and fresh beans we're having for dinner
tonight."

"No calories in fried chicken."

"No cholesterol, either. What the hell, right?" He
smiled sideways at her, a gleam in his pale eyes. "Let's
be sinful and decadent while we can."

She laughed. "I suppose it can't hurt, especially if we
skip dessert—"

"Skip dessert! Perish the thought, woman." He
waved a floury hand behind him. "The cake's atop the
fridge, ready to be iced."

She looked; he wasn't fibbing. "With?"

"Buttercream chocolate frosting, of course. Now out
of my way." He put his hands firmly on her hips and
lifted her up, setting her a foot or so down the counter.

His hands slipped up under her breasts. "We'll break all the rules of clean living tonight, darlin'."

With a wink, he released her and got back to his biscuit dough. "Cal—" She exhaled, cutting herself off. Why break the mood? Why get serious and make her guilty admission now when they could have such a good time together? *Coward*, she chastised herself. But no. She didn't have to tell him anything until tomorrow. Why not leave tonight alone? Make it a memorable last night.

Her throat tightened. A last night. The grand finale. That was exactly what it might be. She would leave for Houston tomorrow, and that very well could be the end of her and Cal.

No. She couldn't imagine that.

"Cal, I have to talk to you."

"Sure."

He got an ancient rolling pin out of a drawer and sprinkled flour all over the counter where she'd been sitting. He'd pushed up the sleeves of his sweatshirt, revealing strong, tanned forearms—was she the only woman who thought forearms were irresistibly sexy— and his hands were caked with flour and bits of dough.

She proceeded. "There's been something I've been wanting to tell you, but I just haven't been able to. Cal, I—" She allowed herself to be distracted by his movements, quick and sure as he rolled out the dough. He got a juice glass from a cupboard above the counter and dipped it in flour. With sharp twists, he cut the biscuit dough into two-inch rounds. She attempted a smile. "Maybe I should wait until after dinner to confess. Those biscuits look as if they're going to be mouth-watering—I'd hate to miss them."

He paused with the glass in midair, giving her a serious look. "Juniper, no matter what you have to tell me, you'll be staying for dinner."

"I won't hold you to that," she said lightly, but her heart was thudding. She wrung her hands, then pulled them apart. To hell with it, she thought. "Cal, I have to go to Houston tomorrow."

He set down the glass and, bending, opened the drawer under the oven and found a slightly warped baking sheet. He placed the biscuit rounds onto it, one by one. "Houston? What for?"

"A job interview."

He froze almost imperceptibly, but she was looking for a reaction. His fingers seemed to stiffen as he finished loading the cookie sheet. He shoved it into the already preheated oven. Then he gathered up the scraps and, with one tanned hand, formed them into a fresh ball of dough. He wasn't looking at Juniper. She considered touching him, making some gesture of affection or reassurance, but decided it would only seem patronizing and empty. She sat very still, waiting for him to say something.

"For a catalog company?" he asked curtly.

"Yes."

"The one that sells those leggings and dragon earrings."

It wasn't a question, but Juniper said, "That's right. They—they're not in direct competition with Killibrew Traders."

He looked at her then, his expression nearly unreadable. If she hadn't known him so well, Juniper would have assumed he didn't give a damn about whether she went to Houston or anywhere else. But she did know him, and behind those placid cornflower eyes she suspected there was a man who was both confused and angry. . . and feeling just a bit betrayed.

"Don't do us any favors," he said tonelessly.

She was strangely comforted, if only fleetingly, by the way he said "us." It indicated to her, perhaps for the first time, that Killibrew Traders was something more to him than just another company, a "them" from which he squeezed a profit and damned little else. But of course they weren't discussing Traders or Calvin Gilliam. They were discussing her.

"The appointment's for the day after tomorrow. At two. I'm leaving tomorrow morning. I'll get a flight out of Bangor."

He looked away. "They'll offer you the job, you know."

"I wouldn't bother going all that way if that weren't a distinct possibility."

"Have you decided what kind of offer you might accept?"

She shrugged, gripping the edge of the counter as she hunched forward. "I haven't decided I'll accept any offer."

"Isn't that bad faith on your part?"

"It's a risk a company takes—and I am going with an open mind."

He rolled out more dough, cut the remaining biscuits and turned and leaned against the counter, so he and Juniper were side by side. "Damn," he said. He threw up his hands and let them flop down at his sides. "All right, then, we're just going to have to work something out."

Juniper nearly slipped off the counter. "Work something—Cal, what are you saying?"

Turning, he settled himself between her knees and held her lightly by the hips. She slipped her arms onto his shoulders and clasped her hands loosely behind his neck.

"I'm saying," he began, measuring each word, "that we have too much that's right between us not to at least *try* to get through the hard parts. I've known they were coming, haven't you?"

She nodded. "I take it, then, you're not mad?"

"Not mad?" He laughed, squeezing her hips. "You've known about this appointment for weeks and haven't bothered to tell me until now. You're making the possibility very real that I'm not going to be able to lure you back to Killibrew Traders under any circumstances. You'll most likely take your talents to a competitor. You might move all the way the hell to Houston—and and you wonder if I'm not mad? Juniper, mad doesn't cover it. Try furious, fit to be tied, wounded to the quick—" He caught his breath, tightening his grip on her. "Try damned determined." His eyes held hers. "I want us to work, Juniper"

Her fingers dug into his shoulders. "So do I, Cal. I can cancel—"

"No. Go to Houston, Juniper. See what the company's like—the city, being away—really away—from Traders, and me. I don't want you to cancel because of me."

"It wouldn't be just because of you, it would be because of us."

He shook his head. "You know that doesn't make sense, don't you? I don't want you to regret later the decision you make now. Go. You have to get on with your life, your career. I can't tell you what you should or shouldn't be doing with your talents. And God knows neither of us would be happy with you playing second fiddle to me or anyone. You have decisions to make, and I want you to make them freely."

"I k-know." She choked on the words.

"Spending the rest of our lives up here in Maine together . . . well, that's just not enough, not for you, not for me. Do you understand what I'm saying?"

"Yes." She smiled and caught a lock of his thick, dark hair with one finger. "You're being a sensitive and caring modern man."

He grinned. "Instead of an eighteenth-century rogue?"

"Oh, you get that out of your system in your business dealings."

"Life is complicated," he said.

"Very."

"I'll drive you to the airport tomorrow."

"You've come a long way from stealing résumés out of my mailbox."

"I was thinking of myself then. Now I'm trying to think of you."

"But maybe I should be thinking of you—"

"Please. I'm the one twisting the guilt knife right now. But if you'll excuse me, the biscuits are about to burn."

He grabbed a pot holder and whisked the tray out of the oven. They weren't burned, but a perfect brown, and they smelled heavenly. He flipped them out into a bowl, covered them with a clean hand towel and piled the unbaked biscuits onto the still hot sheet, promptly shoving them into the oven.

He turned on the faucet and began scrubbing his hands. "One more thing, Juniper."

She was swinging her legs. "Sure, what?"

He pointed a dripping finger at her hips. "I'm afraid I got flour all over you."

She glanced down; he had. "Well, just so long as you don't get any ideas about popping me into the oven."

"Now there's an idea."

And he went for her. Laughing, she scooted down the counter, but didn't get very far with the stove right there. "Don't burn that lovely behind," Cal said, and snatched her up, lifting her off the counter.

She straddled him high, above the waist, and her sweatshirt rode up almost to her breasts. He opened his mouth next to her navel and blew hard, tickling her with his tongue.

"Stop—that tickles!"

He didn't stop and, going for revenge, she pushed her hand under his upper arm and began tickling him. He pulled his mouth from her stomach and spun sharply around yanking her hand out from under his arm as he lifted her higher.

"I could pull your hair, you know," she warned.

He laughed. "You could do worse than that, but you wouldn't."

"Who says?"

"I stand corrected. You would."

He strode across the living room and tossed her down on the couch, then dived on top of her. His hair was wild, his eyes brimming with energy and passion. He was breathing hard. Juniper liked to think of herself as svelte, but she was no lightweight, even for a man as fit as Cal. Yet even though she'd been the one hauled off, she, too, was gasping for air. It was the wanting, she knew—familiar, always there, finally accepted.

"Do worse how—and don't push your luck, Gilliam," she countered.

"You'd never hurt me."

She gave him a look of mock innocence. "I never said I'd pull hard."

He eyed her curiously. "Pull what hard?"

"Your *hair*. You devil—"

His mouth came onto hers, and she responded eagerly, opening her own mouth, searching for his tongue, teasing, probing, wanting. She ached all over for him. She rubbed her tongue along the edge of his teeth, and he lay motionless on her, letting her do as she pleased. But she could feel the hardness of him thrusting up between them, and she flicked her tongue daringly against his then in a primitive rhythm, inviting.

It was all they could stand. He peeled off her sweatshirt, discovered immediately that she was wearing no bra and, with a sharp intake of breath, pounced. With his wet, warm, hungry mouth, he seized one nipple and lapped and sucked and ran his tongue back and forth, faster and faster, only taking time out to go for her pants, until she was thrashing beneath him. They were of the drawstring variety and came off easily, as did her underpants.

He captured her breast again and, lying naked beneath him, she touched his hair ever so lightly. He kissed a hot, wet trail lower and lower, until he came down into the spot that was throbbing for him and repeated what he'd done to her nipples, lapping and tugging and sucking until she was panting and crying out.

Then he sat up, his knees straddling Juniper at the waist, and tore at his jeans until he was free. She took his warm and thrusting shaft into her hands and then, for the first time, into her mouth. She wanted to please him, to feel him throb and shudder with pleasure, and when he did, electricity surged between them.

"What you do to me," he said hoarsely, pulling away.

She laughed. "What we do to each other."

He cast off his sweatshirt, and when he lowered himself back onto her, he entered her at once, thrusting madly, and she responded, pulling him more deeply inside her. He raised himself for a moment, then threw himself even more deeply, faster, harder into her. She cried out in pleasure, and they rolled onto the floor in one motion, not coming apart. Juniper was on top now. She rocked back and forth on him until she was dizzy with ecstasy.

Finally Cal clasped his arms around her back and drew her down onto himself, holding her there while he thrust into her again and again and again, finding his own release.

A while later, when they had caught their breath, wondering at the depth, the sheer energy of their passion for each other, it was Juniper who remembered the biscuits.

"Hell!" Cal leaped up and shot to the oven. But it was too late. The biscuits were burned, a sheet of hard black nuggets. He tossed them into the sink, where the pan sizzled in the spray of cold water.

Leaning against the counter, Cal shook his head at Juniper, who had crawled over to warm herself in front of the fire. "I don't know, Juniper, I doubt I'll ever get enough of you."

Her eyes met his in a look of warmth and loving. "I hope not."

CAL WAITED in the terminal of Bangor International Airport until Juniper's plane had taken off safely. He didn't know what she would find in Houston—neither did she. Answers? It was possible. He knew one thing: he was glad he hadn't mentioned the troubles at Killibrew Traders. Juniper didn't need any additional pressure from him. She had tough decisions to make.

Cal knew that just as he knew, beyond any doubt, that he wasn't going to let her drift away from him, not easily.

"Damn it," he muttered, "we'll just have to work something out."

He returned to the cottage and, piling the dog and two cats he'd promised to feed while she was gone into his car, packed up and headed for Portsmouth. It was time he assessed the damage at his company.

13

THE SMELL of Killibrew Traders wasn't right. The feel of it wasn't right. Whatever the company had had the day of the tulip festival, when Cal had first experienced its special aura, was absent now. Even on paper, things were a mess. Cal spent hours on his first day back closeted with Arthur Green, going over the untenable state of affairs.

Arthur looked like hell, and Cal told him so. With a grim smile Arthur said, "I guess once in the life of every brilliant New York consultant he has to fall flat on his face. I have, Cal."

"You want out?"

"As soon as possible. You back in the saddle?"

Cal sighed. "I guess I don't have a choice."

"I'll stick around as long as I can, but things around here— Well, your Juniper Killibrew just never played by the book. I'm teaching a course next year at NYU. I think I'll have the class do a study of this place. Could be instructive."

Cal just shook his head, barely listening. He'd been wrong about Juniper but, of course, she'd been wrong about him. But was it too late to fix the damage? In frustration he swore silently to himself. Dammit, he didn't want her to take that job in Houston! He could try to tell himself it was her decision, that they could work something out, but he wondered, if their positions were switched, if she would be as understanding.

Ha! "Hell, no," she'd say. "You're not going to drag my butt to Houston, and I don't want a long-distance marriage—"

"Cal?" Arthur sounded worried. "Cal, you okay? You look a bit gray."

Marriage, he thought. Had it come to that? Lord. He no longer knew what to think, except that he wanted Killibrew Traders to thrive and Juniper Killibrew to be a part of his life—and for him to be a part of her life. He didn't want to dictate what she was going to do with herself. He wouldn't—couldn't. So there would be no ultimatums, no, "It's me or Houston." They'd just have to work something out.

"I'm fine," he said, managing a tight smile. "Give me the details, Artie. I want to know everything there is to know about this damned company."

"Onward, huh, Cal?"

"Yes. Onward."

But to what? Victory—or defeat?

THE CATALOG COMPANY was as impressive and interesting as Juniper could have hoped for. Cleverly set up, efficient and staffed with amiable people, it had its offices on two floors of a mirrored-glass building in Greenway Plaza. Juniper liked what she saw during her two-hour tour of the company. It was all so different from Killibrew Traders, but innovative at the same time.

That would be what she would need, wouldn't it? Something very different from what she was used to. It would be easier to forget how very satisfying and challenging her work at Killibrew Traders had been.

And she'd need something different and exciting to keep her from thinking about Cal. She cared deeply about him, wanted him to be happy, wanted to be with him forever. But she didn't know if leaving Killibrew Traders would be a greater threat to their relationship . . . or if staying would be.

That evening she had dinner with the chief executive officer, and he made her an offer that nearly caused her to gulp her wine. It was far more than what she'd made at Traders, for half the work and none of the frustration. This company *had* a working president. No more covering for Summerfield, no more doing his job for him, as well as her own. She could lead the normal life of a working person for a change!

But without Cal there every day. Without annual tulip festivals. Without Beth and all the other people she cared about at Traders. Without Auntie strolling in at all hours for tea and scones. Without unexpected visits from Summerfield. Without her monstrosity of a house.

"That's a very generous offer," she told the CEO. "I'll give it serious consideration."

She returned to the hotel and spent a sleepless night. In the morning, she flew north.

THERE WAS NO ANSWER at Cal's cottage when she called from the Bangor airport. Juniper tried for an hour but finally gave up, rented a car and drove herself to the coast. She was profoundly irritated with him. "All rogues are unreliable," Auntie would have said.

Suddenly Juniper's heart began to pound. What if Cal had a reason for not being at the cottage? What if something terrible had happened while she'd been gone?

What if he'd decided she was a selfish witch and had given up on her? No, she thought, that wasn't Cal. He knew she was confused. He knew she was thinking of him, too, not just herself—didn't he?

When she arrived, she saw that Cal's Mercedes was gone, and Sum's cottage was locked up. Dispirited, she trudged over to her place.

There was a note on her refrigerator. "Juniper," it read, "I took the critters and headed to Portsmouth to assess damages. Duty calls. Figured you're an adult and could manage a ride back from the airport. Talk with you soon. Hope you missed me as much as I'm missing you. C."

Juniper sank into an overstuffed chair near the cold fireplace. The cottage seemed so quiet without Bo and the cats, so empty and desolate without Cal. Or was it just her mood? She loved this place. She would come here again alone some day and relish the solitude.

But not now. All she could think about and feel were the ache and frustration of not having Cal there.

Maine was over, she thought. That had been the easy part, the falling in love with him, the laughter and the lovemaking. Now came the hard part, finding a way they could be together and not swallow each other up.

CAL FOUND SUMMERFIELD whistling away and grilling steaks on the deck of his seaside condominium. "You're happy as a lark," Cal said in an accusing tone.

Summerfield ground fresh pepper on a two-inch T-bone. "I'm being decadent tonight. Haven't had a steak in months—cholesterol, you know." He set down the pepper grinder. "Heard you were in town, Cal, and I can't say I'm disappointed. Hell, if Juniper's going to be a pain in the ass about this thing, you'd better jump in and rescue Traders."

Cal leaned against the deck rail and scowled at Summerfield. "Juniper might not continue to be a 'pain in the ass' if you'd come clean to her."

"Cal—"

"You're established, aren't you?"

"More or less."

"She can't do anything to stop you."

Summerfield took on a look of sheer Killibrew stubbornness. "Not a chance."

"Then for God's sake *tell* her."

"I hear a touch of frustration in your voice, Cal."

"You hear more than a touch, friend. Talk to your niece, or I swear I'll trot her right down to your office and—"

Summerfield threw up his hands, stopping Cal in midsentence. "Okay, okay, I can see this means a lot to you. Is the mess at Traders that bad?"

"It's bad, but that's not why I'm here."

"Juniper?"

"Yes."

Summerfield's jolly look vanished. "Surprise, surprise. Okay, I guess I can't postpone the inevitable forever. I'll try to think of some way of telling her that will keep her from killing me—and you."

"Why the hell should she want to kill me? It was your idea."

"Yeah." Summerfield grinned. "But you kept your word and haven't told her."

"So? That's cost me, not her. She's been thinking I manipulated you into selling out. *I'm* the one who's suffered!"

"Mark my words, Cal. Juniper won't see it that way."

JUNIPER ARRIVED IN PORTSMOUTH the following day at noon and went directly to her house, where her orange door glared in the bright summer sun and Bo was asleep on the porch. It felt good to be home. As she walked inside with Bo, she thought of Houston. Would she be able to duplicate there her life here? A ridiculous question, she realized. This was the house her great-grandfather had built. It was her roots. In Houston, she would have to sink new roots.

But in a way, if she stayed here in New England, she would have to begin anew, as well.

She debated doing a hundred different things, but at the top of her list was walking through the woods to Killibrew Traders to see Cal. Yet she didn't. As much as she wanted to see him and talk to him and just *be* with him, she held back, envisioning him with his sleeves rolled up, papers spread out on his desk, Artie Green pacing in front of him as they discussed her company. Her office would be empty, and she would just be a visitor.

She wasn't ready for that.

So she got out her wallpaper-scraping equipment and filled up her plastic bucket with water and set to work in the living room. She put Beethoven's Seventh on the stereo. In some ways, it was as if she'd never left.

She was singing along with the third movement when a prickly feeling at the base of her neck prompted her to swivel around on her stepladder.

Cal was there, in the doorway. She had no idea how long he'd been standing there watching her. He wore a double-breasted business suit, gray, impeccably tailored. His hair was neatly combed, and his shoes were shiny. Everything about him made him look the part of the harried executive returning home from a long day of work.

And here she was. Waiting for him. How odd, she thought. Could she spend the rest of her life scraping wallpaper and listening to Beethoven?

I'm not the type, she thought. *I'm just not.*

She flicked some gunk off the end of her scraper and sat on the top step of the ladder.

"Well," he drawled, "welcome home."

"Glad to be back."

"Are you?"

"Yes."

"How was Houston?"

"Hot."

The Beethoven was too loud. He walked into the living room—she watched how he moved, remembered the nights they'd spent together—into the dining room and turned down the stereo. He leaned in the doorway.

Juniper made a show of admiring her handiwork with the walls. "At this rate, I might get some paint on by Christmas. Imagine that. Wouldn't a Christmas tree look great in this room?"

He scrutinized her. "Does that mean you intend to be here for Christmas?"

Knowing she owed him an explanation, she nonetheless couldn't bring herself to go into details now, wet and caked with wallpaper and paste the way she was. She slid down off the ladder and laid the scraper on a step. "Let me go up and shower," she said. "I'll explain everything over dinner."

"Do you want me to go with you?"

He spoke in that same deadly-serious drawl, and it took Juniper a few seconds before she heard the sensuality beneath his words . . . and saw it in his expression.

She smiled. "I stink."

"Do you?" He moved toward her then and, expensive suit and all, took her in his arms. "Just a touch rancid."

"It's the old wallpaper paste."

"I'm sure."

They went upstairs together and turned on the shower in her four-legged bathtub that was encompassed by three cheerful yellow shower curtains, which Cal eyed dubiously.

"You don't like yellow?" she asked.

"It'll be hard making love in there."

"We could break our necks, couldn't we?"

"I can see the headlines in the Portsmouth papers now."

"What would our families say?"

He laughed and wrapped his arms around her waist just as she dropped her ratty sweatshirt on the floor. "I don't know, I have a feeling yours would think it's a hell of a way to go."

"Even Auntie?"

"Especially Auntie."

Nevertheless, they didn't try to make love in the shower, but let the water pelt their skin, adding to the tingling sensations of longing, making them moan with desire. They very nearly didn't make it to her room. As they fell into bed, Cal lifted her onto him and eased her down, coming into her. She ended up on top. Raising her chest off his, she moved back and forth on him, shutting her eyes at the ecstasy of being together again.

He touched his hands to her breasts, caressing them, and she opened her eyes. "I missed you," she said, and when he thrust hard into her and slid his arms around her back, she pressed her breasts to the solid wall of his chest.

"If you move to Houston," he murmured, "and we see each other only on weekends, we're going to have some very long, wonderful Saturdays and Sundays."

"And Friday nights," she said, and after that, could say no more.

Afterward, their thirst for lovemaking temporarily quenched, feeling relaxed all over, Juniper helped Cal put supper on the table. He'd made chili the day before—"better use of time than sulking," he said—and they heated that up while putting together a salad. Oddly enough, she thought he looked perfectly at home in her ancient kitchen.

"I suppose this house isn't what you're used to," she said, simply because it was easier than talking about Houston.

Cal nibbled on a radish. "No, but it has lots of possibilities, doesn't it? I'd like to hear what your plans for it are." He waved his paring knife vaguely. "I could buy it from you if you move to Houston."

"Not funny, Cal."

He shrugged. "Neither is trying to avoid the subject. We have to talk, you know."

She admitted reluctantly that he was right, and over dinner told him about her trip. And he admitted that he could understand why she might be tempted. "It would be a fresh start for you—and it's a hell of an opportunity. The company's twice the size of Traders."

"What if I accepted the offer?"

He looked at her. "What if you did?"

"I asked first."

"All right, then, what do you want me to say?"

"That you won't walk out of my life."

"Is that all?"

She nodded, her throat tightening. "Yes."

"I won't walk out of your life, Juniper. Not ever—not for a reason like that. But do you want to know if I'd *like* you going to Houston?"

She sighed. "I don't know if *I'd* like me in Houston. On the one hand, I think we need separate careers. I can't go back to Traders. We could never have an equal partnership—not with you owning the company and me being nothing but an employee. It wouldn't be like it was. Everything would change. And even staying in Portsmouth would be a problem. Everyone knows I've been humiliated—and Summerfield. I can tell he wouldn't be thrilled with the prospect of having me around. Whatever he's up to, he seems to need some space right now, and I guess I do care enough about him that I don't want to get in his way."

Saying nothing, but listening intently, Cal ate his chili. Juniper was grateful he was a man who could listen, even to things he didn't want to hear. He seemed to respect that they were things she didn't much want to say. Was she making any sense at all? She thought so.

"On the other hand—" She broke off with a loud sigh. "On the other hand, Houston isn't exactly down the road, and if you have to stay here and mind shop at Traders—I don't know. We'd be competitors, we'd hardly ever see each other. It just wouldn't be easy. But other people have done it. We could manage—if we wanted to."

Still Cal said nothing.

Juniper ate some chili—spicy, hot, made with chunks of beef instead of hamburger. A man who could make good chili. What more could she want? She gazed down at her spoon. "What do you think?"

"Do you want me to tell you what to do?"

"I want your opinion."

"My opinion." He leaned back in his chair, observing her, and mulled that over. "Do you want the truth, or do you want me to tell you what I think you want to hear?"

She shut her eyes briefly. "The truth."

"All right. The truth is that I can understand how you feel and even sympathize, and I care enough about you not to try to make up your mind for you. Whatever you decide, I can live with it. If I have to sell Traders and move to Houston to be with you, dammit, I'll do it. I don't expect you to toddle after me like a little puppy dog. You have a lot to offer the business world. I don't intend to stop you."

She smiled. "Thanks. That felt good to hear."

He didn't smile back. "But," he said ominously, "I think you're being ridiculous about a few things. One, this 'humiliation' nonsense. Summerfield didn't humiliate you, and neither did I, and when you take the time to gather all the facts, you'll see what I mean. Two, this 'we can't be equal partners' nonsense. Juniper, for God's sake. So I own the company? Big deal. As soon as we're married, it'll be yours, too—"

"Through default."

"Horse manure."

She bit back a hysterical laugh and a wave of giddiness; had he actually thought of marriage as a reality? Had she?

"Listen to me," he went on flatly. "I know our styles and backgrounds and abilities are different, but I see them as complementing each other, not competing with each other. We'd make one hell of a team, Juniper."

"You believe that?"

"I know it." He leaned across the table and, if possible, his look of intensity magnified until she found herself nearly hypnotized, hardly breathing at all. "And I also think it's not just the company," he went on. "It's us. It's my reputation, this 'rogue' nonsense you and your auntie have cooked up. Despite what you know about me, you're still afraid I'll swallow you up somehow, that you'll end up being just an extension of me."

"That's not true."

"Isn't it?"

She thought of her wallpaper scraping and how she'd felt when he'd walked through the door. He'd looked so powerful and in control, whereas she'd felt so helpless. She hadn't before. It was only, she realized, because he was in Traders and she wasn't. He had direction. She didn't.

"When I decide what to do with myself," she said quietly, "that will change."

"But you're afraid it won't change if you stay at Traders."

"Maybe."

"It's just the perception you have of things, Juniper—it's gotten twisted somehow. Have you ever for a single second felt you were just an extension of me with no real value of your own?"

She was appalled. "Of course not!"

"Then why would you—ever? It's a groundless fear." He reached across the table, touching the top of her hand. "But I don't think that's all, or even the biggest part of what's bothering you—and therefore me. You've built a wonderful life here for yourself, and ever since you met me you've had to face the fact that it's changed. Mine has, too, Juniper, and don't think that hasn't scared the hell out of me at times. But as much as we might have liked what we were doing, who we were before we were tossed together, we can't go back to that. That part of our lives is finished. I don't want to go back. I only want to go forward."

Juniper sagged in her chair, feeling confused and, at the same time, reenergized. Rightly or wrongly, Cal had spoken with great caring and empathy, and while she knew she had to come to her own decision, she appreciated his telling her honestly what he thought.

"I guess I just need some time to think this all through," she said.

He nodded, smiling. "Do you want to be alone?"

"Alone?" The thought hadn't occurred to her. "Now, you mean? Good heavens, no."

"Nice to hear."

"Because you had no intention of leaving, anyway?"

He laughed. "Incomparable rogue that I am."

JUNIPER HAD TEA the next morning on the porch and pondered her fate. Cal had left early, irritated with her because she wouldn't walk over to Traders with him. They'd argued, and she could see his frustration with their situation was fast reaching its peak.

"I wish I'd never the hell *heard* of Killibrew Traders," he'd fumed.

She had tried being matter-of-fact. "Then you'd never have met me."

"Don't count on it." His voice had dropped to a low growl as he'd glared at her. "We're fated to be together, Juniper. Remember that."

And he'd stomped off.

An old Mercedes puttered into the driveway, and Juniper glanced up first with curiosity, and then with something approaching dread. It was Auntie. At this time of year, Auntie Killibrew rarely left Mt. Desert Island—not without good reason. Juniper flew to her feet and ran down off the porch, greeting her elderly aunt as she climbed out of the car.

"What on earth are you doing here?" Juniper asked breathlessly. "Is something wrong?"

"On the contrary." Auntie peered at her great-niece from under a wide-brimmed straw hat. "Get in the car, Juniper. We're going somewhere."

"I was just having tea...."

"In."

Perplexed at her aunt's presence and her uncompromising mood, Juniper climbed into the old car. Auntie followed.

"Where are we going?"

"You'll see."

"Don't be mysterious, Auntie."

The old woman smiled enigmatically. "It's one of my finer qualities."

That silenced Juniper, and they talked of other matters, all trivial, until Auntie turned into the rambling, two-thirds-closed plant of Summerfield Shoe on the outskirts of an industrial section of the city.

"Auntie?" Juniper was truly worried now. "Are you all right? Summerfield Shoe ... that hasn't been a family concern in *decades*."

Auntie adopted a look of profound satisfaction and sighed contentedly. "I know."

"You're not going dotty on me, are you?"

"Not yet, my dear. Come along."

They went in a main entrance, down a dim hall, past dusty offices, up a narrow flight of stairs, down another hall and into a sunlit suite of mahogany-trimmed offices. All the furnishings were from the period of Auntie's prime. She seemed quite at home as she escorted Juniper through a door with a frosted-glass window that said Executive Offices.

Summerfield Killibrew was on the telephone behind a massive walnut desk—in the office of the president. He even had a secretary, an efficient-looking woman who had told Auntie and Juniper to go right in.

Looking startled, Summerfield said, "I'll get back to you as soon as I can," and hung up.

Juniper gaped.

Summerfield was on his feet, running a hand nervously through his hair and grinning. "Well, hi. Of all the people I didn't expect here today... Auntie, how are you? Juniper?"

Auntie said she was fine. Juniper continued to gape. Her uncle—her casual, feckless uncle—was wearing a tan business suit, the jacket draped across a chair, his shirt sleeves rolled up, his rep tie loosened. He looked as if he'd been working. He looked serious. He looked happy, and that was the strangest part of all.

"How do you like my new office, June?" he asked innocuously.

"Your new . . . *Summerfield*! What on earth is this?"

"It's Summerfield Shoe," Auntie replied for him.

"I know that much," Juniper snapped. "But what are you doing here? Summerfield . . . you're not . . . you haven't *bought* the company, have you?"

"Lock, stock and barrel." He beamed. "And I intend to turn it around."

"The American shoe industry is in dire straits! How can you expect—"

"High-quality products and walking," Summerfield said proudly. "Believe me, Juniper, I know exactly the state of the shoe industry, but Summerfield Shoe has always had a good reputation for its products—if not its management. We're building our new base on our high-quality walking shoe. Walking's the new big exercise craze, you know, and it cuts right across the generations—just about anyone can walk. And I'm going to be right there with the best shoe."

Juniper shook her head, not at what he was saying, but in shock. "Summerfield, I've never seen you so excited."

He smiled. "I've never been so excited. I've been working night and day getting this thing rolling, and I love every minute of it—every miserable little detail. It's the first time I've ever really understood you, too, Juniper. What pushes you, how you could derive so much pleasure from your work."

"So this is what selling Traders was all about. Cal didn't go to you—you went to him." Juniper sighed and looked over at her great-aunt. "You knew?"

"Knew?" Auntie scoffed. "I put him up to it."

"That's a bit of an overstatement," Summerfield said with a laugh. "Auntie knew I'd been itching to strike out on my own, do something different, make an impact. When she told me *her* dream of reviving Summerfield Shoe— Well, everything just came into place."

"And you didn't feel you could tell me," Juniper said sadly.

"I didn't want your interference, but mostly, I guess, I didn't want your advice. I wanted to do this on my own, Juniper. I'm sorry if I hurt you."

She turned to her aunt. "And you didn't tell me."

"Couldn't," Auntie said without guilt. "I made a promise to Summerfield and couldn't break it. I'd have done the same for you. You know that. I admit I wasn't too sure about this Calvin Gilliam fellow at first, but as it is, I think you've both behaved like imbeciles. Well, now the cat's out of the bag. The question is, what are you going to do about it?"

"I don't know."

"Whatever it is," her uncle said, "I'll support you, Juniper. It's the least I can do."

Auntie sighed impatiently. "Come along, Juniper. We've dillydallied here long enough. You can come back for a tour another time."

"What do you mean? Auntie—"

"Well," she said starchily, "do you or don't you want to get to Killibrew Traders before that Arthur Green and your Calvin Gilliam make any more of a mess of things? For heaven's sake, Juniper, they *need* you!"

Juniper had to laugh. "Let's go."

Cal was at the desk in Summerfield's old office, running one hand through his dark hair, a pained expression on his striking face. Seeing him, Juniper felt a rush of tears. Emotion, she thought. She loved this man. Adored him, wanted him, just plain *liked* him. And it was time to stop even considering that she could live without him. Oh, she could—people did survive monumental loss. But she didn't have to. She didn't want to.

"I've been to see Summerfield," she blurted out, feeling out of place in her yellow jumpsuit. She should be working, dammit! "He told me everything."

Cal put down his pen and pushed the report he was reading to the center of his desk. He looked less pained. "It's about time."

"I probably should be furious with you," she said. "You could have told me sooner. I'd cast you as the bastard in this business right from the start—and me and Summerfield as the victims. And of course that's not true. There are no villains and no victims."

"I couldn't have told you, Juniper. I'd promised Sum—long before I'd met you."

She came around to him and sat on the edge of his desk, her calves touching his thighs. The longing was there, familiar but welcome now. "I know. Your friendship with Summerfield and your loyalty to him are just further proof of the kind of man you really are, Cal. You're exciting, decent, fascinating and a good and true friend. I admire that." She paused. "As for the decision about what *I'll* do next . . . Well, Auntie tells me Killibrew Traders needs me. I think I agree with her."

He gave her a dry look, but he was thrilled; she could see it in his eyes. "You always have had a clear view of your virtues, haven't you? Of *course* Traders needs you! Sum explained the ungodly mess we're in—"

She shot to her feet. "Ungodly mess? I expected things to be a bit unsteady around here without me, but is it that bad? Cal— Dammit, Gilliam, what have you been keeping from me?"

He slid back in his chair, just out of reach of her fists. "Now calm down. I wouldn't have sprung it on you like that, except I assumed Sum had already entertained you with all the gory details." He quickly—and baldly— outlined the pertinent facts of the problems that had beset Killibrew Traders since he'd become owner and Juniper had resigned. "I accept full responsibility, of course. If I had paid more attention to what was going on here and less to trying to woo you back, none of this need have happened."

Although she was shaken by just how bad affairs were, Juniper only frowned at Cal and asked, "Then I assume things are falling into place now that you're at the helm."

"Actually—no. You said it best: Traders needs you."

She leaned back against the desk and folded her arms over her breasts. "I can't say I'm surprised."

His eyes narrowed. "You're taking a fiendish delight in all this, aren't you?"

"Absolutely."

"What's the word for a female rogue?" He was on his feet. "Enough's enough, Juniper. Tell me what I have to do to get you to stay—before I start eliminating my own guesses one by one."

She fingered his slate blotter. "Give me half of Killibrew Traders—in black and white, so I know it's mine and no one can take it away, no matter what."

"*Half!*"

"Fifty percent. There should always be a Killibrew at Killibrew Traders, don't you think?"

"You pirate!"

"Then we'll be equal partners for sure."

"You drive a hard bargain." He moved in closer to her. "What if I don't want you for half?"

She shrugged. "There's always Houston. I can visit you every other weekend."

"And what would I do between visits?"

"Try to sort things out here. Scrape wallpaper. Have dinner with Bo and the cats."

"A devil, that's what you are."

She grinned right into his cornflower eyes. "How do you think I got to where I am today?"

"Genes," he snapped. "You're your Grandpa Killibrew all over again."

Her expression was unrepentant, if not downright cocky.

He laughed. "You're itching to get back to work here, aren't you?"

She could feel his breath warm on her face. "After the mess you've made, I don't know—"

"Ha! I can see the thrill of the challenge in your eyes, Juniper Killibrew. You've got it, too. You're a Killibrew, all right."

"Do I get half up front or not?"

He stood back, appraising her with the cool look of the consummate executive. "It's a deal. Half the company—but on one condition."

"Only one?"

"Yes."

"Name it."

"We get married."

Her breath caught. "When?"

He laughed, then he was there, taking her into his arms. "As soon as we can," he murmured. "I love you, Juniper. I've wanted you from the moment I saw you, and I began loving you the moment you spoke to me. You're beautiful and cantankerous and intelligent and wonderful. There's never been anyone in my life like you. There never will be."

"Cal, you know I love you."

"But I'll never get tired of hearing you say so. I want to make love with you and scrape wallpaper and feed the animals and paint that damned door and work here with you—just live my life with you, forever."

"We have so much we can learn from each other. But you know how hectic our lives will be?"

"I have an idea. And I think that's exactly what we both want. Don't you?"

"Absolutely. We'll both rise to the challenge."

His mouth moved closer to hers. "Don't we always?"

IF GEORGIA BOCKOVEN CAPTURED YOU ONCE, SHE'LL DO IT AGAIN!

In Superromance #246, *Love Songs*, Amy had to protect her friend, Jo, from all the Brad Tylers of the world. Now in Temptation #161, *Tomorrow's Love Song*, Amy has her own troubles brewing....

She assumes a false identity and sets out to right a few wrongs. She's got everything to gain—millions of dollars. And everything to lose—the one man who belongs in her future....

Look for Temptation #161, *Tomorrow's Love Song*. Coming to you in July!

ATTRACTIVE, SPACE SAVING BOOK RACK

Display your most prized novels on this handsome and sturdy book rack. The hand-rubbed walnut finish will blend into your library decor with quiet elegance, providing a practical organizer for your favorite hard-or soft-covered books.

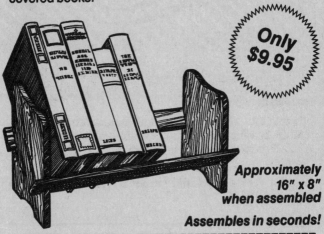

Only $9.95

Approximately 16" x 8" when assembled

Assembles in seconds!

To order, rush your name, address and zip code, along with a check or money order for $10.70* ($9.95 plus 75¢ postage and handling) payable to *Harlequin Reader Service*:

Harlequin Reader Service
Book Rack Offer
901 Fuhrmann Blvd.
P.O. Box 1396
Buffalo, NY 14269-1396

Offer not available in Canada.

BKR-1A

*New York and Iowa residents add appropriate sales tax.

Take 4 best-selling love stories FREE

Plus get a FREE surprise gift!

Harlequin Temptation

COMING NEXT MONTH

#165 THE ULTIMATE SEDUCTION
Madeline Harper

Liza knew that a nibble of chocolate recreated the feeling of being in love—her exclusive chocolate shop wasn't called The Ultimate Seduction for nothing. But then Mac Davidson tempted her with the real thing. . . .

#166 THE IVORY KEY Rita Clay Estrada

That she wasn't alone at her island haven was only the first surprise Hope had to face. Armand Santeuil, her *very* unexpected guest, had many more revelations for her. . . .

#167 BESIEGED Faye Ashley

Two small children, one large Saint Bernard and feisty Cara North equaled trouble for Josh Quinlan. Not only had they disturbed the serenity of his country estate, but Cara was wreaking havoc with his senses. . . .

#168 CHANCE OF A LIFETIME
Jayne Ann Krentz

Abraham Chance had no time for whiners and weaklings. Well, Rachel Wilder was neither— it took guts to plot against the devastating Mr. Chance. And the closer she got to her victim, the more eager she was to add seduction to the game plan. . . .